Don't Wake The Moon

A Supernatural Horror of Lost Children

A G Nuttall

I would like to dedicate this book to my wonderful children,
Oliver and Isabelle.

Chapter One

My name is Valencia Agostini, Leni to my friends and family. I am the youngest child of Sophie and Angelo, an unremarkable couple who work low-income jobs and long hours to pay the bills and put food on the table.

Our apartment in downtown Manhattan is tiny, too warm in the summer and too cold in the winter. My bedroom walls possess an artistic growth of mold that diversifies each year. The room has one captivating quality, though: if you look really hard, you can just make out the Statue of Liberty from my window.

My older brother, Alfie, swaggers around the neighborhood like a Sicilian Don, parading the streets in silk shirts and gold chains, smoking roll-ups with his friends, and dreaming of a life he will most likely never achieve. Alfie refuses to follow in our father's footsteps; factory work is not good enough for him. Hard work and honesty have no place in Alfie's world. Where he makes the money to buy his expensive shirts, I dare not ask, though I suspect it involves something distasteful.

I was born on a cold, damp evening, the night before Halloween. Whether that bears any significance to the fact that I can converse with the dead, I'm not certain. I view my ability as a 'gift' and not a 'curse.'

As far back as I can remember, people of all ages, gender, color, and size accompanied me through daily life. I viewed their presence as normal; I grew not to fear them and eventually found comfort in their existence.

At night, I would share my room with a ghostly vision, sometimes more than one.

An elderly man in a cloth cap and an overcoat occupied the empty space at our dining room table, and a young woman with curly hair and sad eyes sat in the living room each evening as we watched TV.

They were peaceful souls patiently waiting for entry to the afterlife. Unfinished business held them between dimensions. Some made contact, others did not.

Using images, objects, and sometimes their voices, they would endeavor to communicate. If I could decipher their messages, I could help them crossover, and most did successfully. Those left behind became desperate, their messages distorted and jumbled, and they wandered in aimless solitude. I could do nothing to help them.

The older I got, the more adept at communicating I became. I now lived in a surreptitious world, a double life fleeting between the living and the dead. I never discussed any of it in front of my family, who lived in the comfortable denial that I had simply 'grown out of it.'

In High School, I made a small group of friends, Priscilla Roxborough, aka Roxy, and Connie Hart, my two besties. We spent much of our free time together, and both readily accepted my formidable ability, for which they labeled me 'cool.'

Roxy, with a cascade of blond curls and blue eyes, was beautiful, fashion-conscious, and curvy. Guys salivated in her presence, but Roxy never seemed to notice.

Connie, with her flame-colored pixie bob haircut and green eyes, was desperate for male company, though her boyish figure and multiple tattoos didn't seem to attract the Ivy League hopefuls she hungered for.

Finally, there's me, dark—almost black—long, wavy hair and almond eyes. Italian looks with the love of food to match, no self-will, and a constant battle with unwanted calories. I fluctuate between a size four and six depending on mood and gym visits.

Chapter Two

Despite my many visitations and communication with wandering spirits, I never felt afraid or threatened by their presence until the day I visited my grandmother's neighbor.

In the summer holidays, I was visiting with Noni (the Italian name for grandmother). A lively, petite Sicilian woman with a fiery disposition, whose life was spent entertaining family and cooking up a gourmet feast in the kitchen. Noni was always great fun to be around, and I loved spending time with her.

She lived in Sweet Water Bay, Connecticut, an idyllic suburb just a short commute from New York City.

The chasm between homesteads was huge, and I welcomed the frequent escapes. The claustrophobic size of our apartment compared to the rambling expanse of Noni's historic abode served as a welcome relief.

No one knew how Noni and Grandpa Luigi had afforded such an affluent home, and no one was ever brave enough to ask. Rumors took flight when the house was bequeathed to them from an unknown benefactor, though that left more questions than answers.

Whatever the origins of its existence, I loved it. It was spacious and quirky. Spread across three floors, it boasted five bedrooms, two living rooms, a dining room, a family kitchen, a study, six bathrooms, a huge attic, and an enormous basement. Outside, an immense expanse of garden reached far into the distance, stopping only where the horizon nestled above the tree line of neighboring woodland.

It was beautifully decorated with Italian influences, from the oversized furniture and luxurious drapes and cushions, to the ornate fireplaces and the plethora of family photographs. In the winter, its fireplaces roared to life, and in the summer, Noni's kitchen supplied jugs of homemade lemonade and ice cream to help combat the soaring temperatures outside.

I loved the house so much that Noni promised it would be mine when she passed away, but Noni had an abundance of grandchildren all vying for the prize.

I was thirteen at the time and entering the alarming phase of puberty. Noni's house was the only place I felt relaxed, and I had pestered my mom to let me visit for a couple of days.

It was late one afternoon when Noni asked me to deliver a food parcel to her next-door neighbor. Noni said the lady had been unwell and had no family, which to an Italian is unthinkable. Family is like oxygen: necessary and abundant.

"Mind your manners, Leni," she warned as I left the kitchen with the basket of food. I nodded and set off for the house next door, which was a five-minute walk across a vast lawned area and a short length of sidewalk.

I stood at the bottom of the driveway surveying the neighbor's home. It was every bit as big as Noni's and built around the same era, but unlike Noni's, it wore a look of disrepair. A disheveled, decaying monument of a bygone age.

I crossed the driveway, passing an old Chevy, which looked equally as tired and neglected as the cobblestones it sat on.

I knocked timidly, making little impact on the large, weather-beaten door, its occupant unaware of my existence.

I knocked again, harder this time, until my knuckles were red and stinging.

Eventually, a wrinkled, leathery face appeared. It belonged to a rather unfortunate old woman. I say unfortunate as she possessed all the physical attributes of a character from a child's nightmare, namely a witch of the very ugliest kind. I couldn't help but stare. Thick, wiry, gray hair was stacked precariously in a disheveled bun on top of her head. Her nose, though wartless, was misshapen and bulbous. She hovered in the shadow of the doorway, displaying only her side profile.

It was only as she stepped aside and beckoned me to enter that the full horror of her features became visible. The old woman only had one eye. A wrinkled patch of discolored skin masked the hole where the missing eye once sat. The remaining eye was a milky white, making sight for her quite an accomplishment.

The hallway was dimly lit, cold, and silent. Carved statues lurked in shadowy corners like timid children. The skeletal remains of a once exquisite staircase rose to the height of a large skylight, suffocating beneath layers of dirt and leaves. Only the moaning timbers of the house's aging carcass could be heard creaking above the quietude. The signs of neglect were not only restricted to the exterior; the splendor of its original state was also entombed from centuries of disregard.

I had never before entered a home so devoid of emotion, so aesthetically dead, and it was deeply unnerving. I sensed no happiness had lived there; no laughter or music had bounced off the walls. The house was just a soulless chasm as grotesque as its occupant.

The old woman reached for the food basket and disappeared. She returned with a glass of lemonade and signaled for me to follow her down the hall.

We entered a room that resembled a museum for African antiquities. Masks, spears, and shields lined the walls, while animal hooves, heads, and tusks were displayed in shrine-like splendor above the fireplace. Jars of black liquid lined the top of a dark wooden cabinet, and what appeared to be shrunken heads dangled from each side of the old woman's chair. I imagined, and hoped, that they were fakes.

It was the most intriguing place and, at the same time, the creepiest one too.

Beside the fireplace sat the coiled body of a taxidermized cobra. The old woman retrieved a poker from its center and nudged a dying fire back to life. She sidled into her seat and closed her eye.

Not a single word had passed between us, and now only the hiss and crackle of newly awakened embers broke the silence.

"Been to Africa?" I asked in a desperate bid to break the awkwardness.

"No," she replied, her voice as old and decrepit as the rest of her.

"Why d'ya have all these African decorations then?"

"Ask a lot of questions, don't ya, child," scowled the old woman.

I thought I'd only asked two, but I apologized anyway.

The woman glared at me with her one misty eye but said nothing more. It was an uncomfortable situation, and I sipped at the glass of lemonade to shroud my unease. I desperately wanted to bid her farewell, but manners and Noni's judgmental voice ringing in my ears forbade it.

As time passed, the contents of my glass drained, and the old woman appeared to have drifted into sleep. Unsure whether I should leave or stay, I opted to remain for a further five minutes and then release myself from this silent prison.

As I waited impatiently for the minutes to tick by, my eyes were drawn around the unusual room once more, this time settling on the growth of mysterious haze that was forming behind the old woman's chair. It grew slowly and silently, enveloping the old woman as she slept. At first, I thought it was surplus smoke from the fireplace, but the swirling mist hung exclusively around the sleeping crone.

Within the density of the smoky cloud, I sensed the presence of a man. He wore a morning suit and a black top hat decorated with bones and feathers. His features were partially obscured from view, but there was the trace of white paint standing prominent against his dark skin tone, as though he wore a mask. His presence was intimidating; I had experienced nothing quite like it before. He wreaked of death, but mostly of misery and pain. Evil seeped from within him, and his soul was black. He wasn't a man, though he wore the façade. He was something unholy.

I sat transfixed, every muscle plagued with spasms, unable to move, unable to leave.

Suddenly, the old woman sprang forward, her grotesque features piercing the thick, gray haze, as she released a gut-wrenching scream and sank back into her chair. The presence rose above her, and in an instant it and the cloud of mist had dissipated.

I raced from the house, my heart beating rapidly within my chest, and headed back to the safety of Noni, not knowing or caring whether the old woman was dead or alive. I rushed through the kitchen red-faced and breathless, leaving Noni with unanswered questions. I couldn't say anything of my experience; my explanation would be unbelievable, and I wasn't even sure what had happened myself. I never visited the old woman again, and I certainly didn't intend to step back inside her macabre home. That was until many years later when I was invited to dinner.

Chapter Three

Noni died in the summer of 2012, a stroke, they said, though the funeral director was reticent to let me see her body. I couldn't work out why, and that bothered me.

As promised, she had left the suburban house to me. I was only twenty and working at the local news office as a typist.

Desperate to escape the confines of my tiny city bedroom, I convinced Roxy and Connie to move into the house with me; it was far too big for one person, and the extra money would be helpful. On moving day, there was much excitement and a little sadness too. The memories of Noni's smiling face echoed through the house, and it was difficult to imagine I would never enjoy the aroma of her famous Sicilian pasta or hear her raucous laughter again.

I opted for Noni's room, where her bottles of scent still stood in regimented order on the dressing table, and handfuls of costume jewelry hung from the mirror.

Images of her lay everywhere, and I felt comfort from having her things around me. I squeezed my clothes into the wardrobe next to hers and slept on the pillows where she had lain, a faint whiff of her signature scent warming my nostrils as I drifted into sleep.

When the boxes were empty, the wine began to flow as we toasted our new home and Noni's generosity. Life as an independent woman was exciting, and living with my two besties made it even better. We settled into daily life quickly, sharing chores and cooking duties. Every night, we gathered around the kitchen table to eat, drink wine, and chat, in true Italian style.

Three months later, the wreck of the home next door went up for sale. It was a great relief to know that the old woman residing there had either died or entered a home.

The place was sold within a week, and after a multitude of renovations, an all-American family moved in.

I could breathe easily now, and the unexplained memories of my visit there could finally be forgotten.

The house would start a new chapter for the Richards family: Chase, Marie, Tate, and Victoria. Its façade had been wrestled into the twenty-first century, and I was certain that its new owners would treat it with the love and respect it deserved.

Chase was a physician at the local hospital, while Marie was a stay-at-home mom. Tate, aged fifteen, was Marie's son from a previous marriage, and Victoria, almost five, was their first child together.

They cut the shape of a loving, caring family. Chase, the dedicated doctor, worked long, arduous hours in the NICU, where he cared for newborn babies who needed specialist attention.

Marie left the house several times a day, ferrying the kids to extracurricular activities, shopping, and lunching with friends.

Tate was shy and pubescent. He rarely acknowledged our presence, and on the occasion that it was impossible to pass us by without a nod or a wave, he would grunt teenage speak, which we took to represent 'hey.'

A month later, when everyone's routine was operating like the cogs in a well-oiled machine, Marie invited us round for dinner. I was excited to survey the remodeling of the African-themed dwelling and accepted her invitation gladly.

The night before the proposed dinner, I was abruptly awoken by Connie shaking my arm with a sense of urgency.

"Leni, come quickly," she whispered, "there's someone in the little girl's bedroom."

I hauled myself out of bed and staggered wearily across the landing.

Connie had discovered that her bedroom window sat opposite Victoria's, and they often exchanged bedtime waves.

I stared at the window, darkened by the shadows of night, as Connie danced around me in desperation.

"He was standing there at her window looking at me," she shrieked.

"It was probably her daddy or Tate; they are the only men in that house." I tried to reassure her that what she thought she had seen was no cause for concern, and then she threw forth an exploding sentence that shattered my entire body into a state of momentary panic.

"But Leni, he was wearing a top hat."

I sank onto Connie's bed, head spinning at her unexpected revelation.

"You okay? You're shaking," Connie enquired.

I pulled it together and painted on a smile. "Probably the result of sleep deprivation," I mocked, "now get back to bed, and next time your imagination works overtime in the middle of the night, keep it to yourself."

"You don't believe me, do you?"

"If that's what you think you saw, then I believe you, but the mind can play tricks, Connie. Under the shadow of darkness, it's easy for the brain to misinterpret what the eye thinks it sees."

My words were of little comfort, but she accepted them anyway and snuggled beneath the duvet.

Sleep did not find me until dawn, Connie's words weighing heavy on my mind. Before I knew it, the alarm was buzzing beside me, and daylight flashed across the bedroom.

I longed for Noni to make contact, but the fact that she hadn't was also comforting. Noni must have crossed over immediately, and that was a welcoming thought.

CHAPTER FOUR

We threw on our best jeans and favorite tops, a palette of makeup, and a spritz of perfume, and headed to the Richards' house.

Connie brought flowers, Roxy red wine, and I brought a basket of homemade cookies.

Marie answered the door and invited us inside. She accepted our gifts gratefully and offered us a tour of the house.

Its design could not have been more different from the African mausoleum it had replaced. The ground floor was now open plan with marble tiles, neutral-painted walls, and light bouncing through every window. The furniture was modern and minimalist, with not the slightest hint of a shield or spear or shrunken head. A lively fire danced in the center of a dividing wall, throwing out warmth in all directions.

The house felt alive at last. The breath of laughter and love had awoken its soul. Its heart pulsed to the beat of music, its spirit had certainly returned, and yet beneath the positivity I still sensed a strange unease.

Upstairs, the bedrooms were equally spacious and continued in a modern theme. Each one was equipped with a dressing room and a separate bathroom.

We stopped at Victoria's room, where the little girl was happily playing with a wooden doll house.

She had chosen pink and purple decor, her favorite colors, to adorn the walls. A beautiful Cinderella-style carriage posed as her bed set upon a thick white rug in the center of the room. It was every little girl's dream.

As we turned to leave, I noticed an oddity hanging from the canopy of the elaborate bed frame. Marie, realizing the object had grabbed my attention, stated, "Hideous, isn't it? But she would insist on keeping it."

I recognized the shriveled, wrinkled features of the shrunken head immediately. It had hung from the right arm of the old woman's chair and was slightly smaller in size than its counterpart...

"We found it among the few belongings that were left in the house," advised Marie.

I wanted to grab it and burn it, to keep it as far away from Victoria as possible. Such an indelible relic could only mean one thing, and it wouldn't be good.

"I can't imagine you kept anything else," I said, with my fingers firmly crossed, "I once had the displeasure of visiting this house in my youth; your tastes could not have been more different."

Marie laughed, "What was left still lives in the attic; we just haven't had time to go through it all yet."

My heart sank at her words, but I smiled politely and changed the subject.

Chase joined us in the dining room with goblets of wine and pre-dinner delicacies. Tate skulked in his bedroom and only made an appearance when the smell of food lured him to the table.

We took our places for dinner, chatting and laughing with our new neighbors. Discussing Chase's excellent work at the hospital and the wonderful makeover they had given the house.

"I applaud what you've done with the place; it's a definite improvement," I said with a smirk.

"So, you were lucky enough to see the monstrosity we paid good money for," joked Chase, "I can't begin to tell you what an ordeal it was to get rid of that nightmare interior, but Marie, fortunately, has a super eye for design."

"It looks wonderful," stated Roxy, "not that I saw it before, but Leni told me all about it and the old lady who lived here."

"What happened to her?" I enquired.

"Cora Hempell went into a nursing home a month before we bought the place."

"Oh really, I wasn't sure whether she had died."

"Well, she has now," added Marie, "a week after she moved there, she was found dead in bed."

"How awful," stated Connie, "I suppose she was very old."

"Here's the thing though," muttered Chase after checking that Victoria was not within earshot, "they found her with her eye missing and her mouth sewn together. Autopsy could not determine her cause of death."

The room fell silent. A shudder coasted down my spine, tingling every vertebra along the way as the face of the old woman I had tried so hard to forget was suddenly there in front of me.

"Well, that was a conversation stopper," mused Chase as he headed off for another bottle of wine.

Marie served delicious food, and Chase topped up drinks with increasing regularity. Conversation was relaxed, and even Tate contributed a teenage word or two. Victoria was a charming little girl, bubbly in nature, with curly blond hair and bright blue eyes.

As Marie disappeared to dish up apple pie in the kitchen, conversation around the table was flowing as easily as the wine.

Chase, as charming as he was handsome, had Roxy and Connie salivating at his every word.

Tate had disappeared into the world of *Gran Turismo* on his iPad, and I was busily admiring Marie's color scheme and her ability to match several color palettes successfully.

My eyes bounced around the room and settled on Victoria. The little girl was happily engaged in the story of *Snow White and the Seven Dwarfs*.

I was just about to speak to her when I spied a cloud of gray mist gathering behind where she sat. Was the fire smoking? I checked, but the flames of the lively fire were contained behind glass. That wasn't the explanation. Suddenly, I felt anxious as I recalled my visit with the old woman. My throat became dry, and sweat began to form across my forehead as I expected the man in the top hat to appear in the room.

Victoria and the others were happily unaware of the gathering cloud and my increasing trepidation.

The haze began to evaporate, and the outline of a young boy emerged.

The blurred image of a five- or six-year-old grew visibly clearer.

I jumped backwards, a reflex action sending the dining chair clattering beneath me.

"Too much wine, Leni?" Roxy quizzed.

I nodded in agreement and adjusted my seat, apologizing for the sudden outburst.

Connie touched my arm thoughtfully as I trembled beneath the cover of the marble table, my eyes transfixed on the spirit that had joined us.

Standing directly behind Victoria, the little boy stretched out his arm and pointed at the back of her head.

That alone did not disturb me, but his pitiful appearance did. The child was missing both eyes, black, cavernous holes in their place, and his mouth was sewn together with thick black twine. I sensed his agony. The tortuous loss of his sight and the cruel captivity of his voice were disturbing. The child had suffered in the most unimaginable way.

I shuddered at his pain.

"Seen a ghost?" mused Marie.

"Or is it the apple pie?" smirked Chase.

I stared down at the sweet delight in front of me, unaware of its arrival, speechless but smiling. The pie was divine, but my mind was elsewhere.

"You okay, Leni?" enquired Roxy, "you've gone awfully pale."

I nodded, "Too much of this good stuff," I answered, pointing towards the large balloon of red wine.

Conversation continued to flow around me, no one aware of the young guest that had crashed the party with his frightening appearance.

I glanced back to where he had stood, but the child had vanished.

He had unfinished business. His ill-timed appearance was the first attempt at communication, and I hadn't seen the last of him.

I could hardly contain my relief as the evening came to a close, and we left the Richards' home with the promise of a revisit.

"What did you see in there?" urged Roxy as we reached the sidewalk.

"If I tell you, you won't sleep tonight," I replied cautiously.

"Is there anything we can do to help?"

"Do you think it involves the man in the top hat?" Connie proffered.

Roxy threw a questioning glance towards her; the incident of the man in the top hat had not been openly discussed.

Connie inhaled deeply, realizing Roxy was unaware of her encounter, "Well, the other night I…"

"I'm not sure," I interrupted, cutting Connie short, "I need to figure out who I saw and why. There's something in that house; I can feel it... and it's something bad!"

Chapter Five

Connie's description of the man in the top hat, followed by the untimely appearance of the ghostly child in the Richards' dining room, was troubling. I was certain that the spirit wanted to make contact. His appearance behind Victoria indicated that he was there because of her, but *why* was the question. I was certain he was trying to tell me something, and I felt the need to investigate further.

I took a trip to the Town Hall and searched the name of Cora Hempell. I didn't know what I would find, but I thought she was a good place to start.

Her recent obituary stated 'reason unknown' as her cause of death but held little else of interest. I noted the coroner was Dr Curtis Patton; he could be a useful source of information, but first, I decided to pay Cora a visit. Cora's grave was easy to find, the freshly turned earth and sparse covering of grass indicative of her recent interment. A simple tombstone engraved with her name and dates was all that remained of Cora Hempell's 98-year existence.

To the right of her sat the tombstone of Baxter Hempell, who I suspected to be her late husband. To the left was the grave of a third Hempell, aged six. I could only assume that the three of them were somehow related. Perhaps a visit to the local library would be helpful.

Sweet Water library had yet to enter the realms of twenty-first-century technology. Rolls of aging microfiche on a large, manually operated machine were the only way to search for information. To say the process was time-consuming and laborious was an understatement. Before I knew it, the afternoon had passed into evening, and the librarian was waiting to close up. With one roll of film left to view, I pleaded with her for an extra half hour. The promise of a mocha latte saw her reluctantly agree.

Fortunately, I hit the jackpot.

Cora had met Baxter at Cornell University. They married, and Baxter took his wife's surname. I learned that Baxter was a Nigerian immigrant; perhaps the name change was his attempt at blending into American society. Nevertheless, an American woman and an African man was a rare sight in an opinionated homestead like Sweet Water, and the Hempells were far from welcome.

They lived a solitary existence; friends and relatives were scarce, except for Baxter's grandfather, who appeared to live with them.

Baxter became a successful author, and Cora, though highly qualified herself, could only find employment as a seamstress. Both worked from home, hiding their relationship behind thick velvet drapes and dirty windows.

When Cora fell pregnant, they welcomed a little boy, who apparently became the focus of their existence.

The microfiche spluttered, jumping forward a couple of years. The Hempells had hit the headlines with the sudden disappearance of their only child. The child had just turned six.

A rigorous manhunt ensued, but the child was never found. Locals considered Baxter Hempell to be responsible for the boy's demise, though he was never charged.

I removed the film and handed it safely to the librarian.

"Did you find everything you were looking for," she quizzed as I headed for the exit.

"Maybe, though, I have a feeling I will be back."

"Well, I'll be here waiting for my latte," she smiled.

The following evening, I kept my promise and delivered a steaming hot mocha latte.

"I've pulled these films out for you," the librarian told me. "They kinda follow on from the year you finished looking at yesterday. We have the full history of Sweet Water Bay on film if you need it?" The sentence seemed more of a question, as if she wanted to know what my interest was but didn't want to ask directly.

"That's great, thank you. I'll take a look at this one and let you know."

I set off in the direction of the antiquated microfiche reader, then quickly backtracked towards the librarian. Something was drawing me towards her: an impulsion, a knowing, a shared gift.

"You already know what I'm looking for, don't you, Sonia?"

She lifted her eyes to meet mine, her cheeks flushing uncomfortably.

"How could I possibly..."

"The same way I know you're called Sonia."

She reached for her name badge, but it wasn't there; she had forgotten to attach it, and it was sitting on the passenger seat of her red Camaro.

Sonia became flustered, "How...?"

"Your grandmother is standing beside you; she told me your name and where you left your badge."

Sonia adjusted her steel-rimmed spectacles, her eyes wide and her pupils dilated.

"You see them too?"

"I do." Those two little words made quite an impression on Sonia. Her shoulders dropped, and she sank back into her chair and smiled as relief engulfed her.

"You are not alone, Sonia. There are more of us out there than you can imagine."

The first few frames of microfiche held nothing of interest, but then...

Sweet Water Bay headlines were ablaze with reports of missing children. I counted nineteen, missing over a period of ten years from the Bay area and surrounding communities. The police had no leads, no suspects, and no idea what happened to the children, as none of them were ever found. I couldn't help but think of the disfigured child I had encountered the other night. Was he one of the missing children? Whatever the answer, I had a deep impulsion to investigate. He had visited me for a reason. Could this be it?

I made a list of the names, ages, and dates the children went missing; then I invited Sonia for coffee.

Chapter Six

The following weekend, Sonia visited Noni's house; I still couldn't get used to calling it anything else.

She had offered to help investigate the missing children, and in return, I offered to help her understand the gift she had struggled to acknowledge for so long.

She had tried hard to keep her difference hidden away, ignoring the spiritual visitors that had contacted her. She threw herself into church activities, hoping her visions would disappear.

"It doesn't work like that," I told her. "Ignoring it doesn't mean it will go away. You should embrace it... consider yourself special. Not everyone gets to communicate with the dead."

"That's what scares me, Leni. I'm afraid of my own shadow, always have been, so talking to the dead is not something I'm comfortable with."

"Think of yourself as a conduit for someone who has unfinished business. You could help that person resolve whatever is keeping them here, allowing them to pass over peacefully."

"I hadn't thought of it like that, but I can live with that definition," she smiled.

"You're just a detective, but for the dead, not the living. Speaking of which, let's get down to business."

I divided the missing children into two groups, local and out-of-town. Sonia began work on the local list, and I took the other one.

Tracing relatives of children who had been missing for decades was not going to be easy, but Sonia had a secret weapon. Her brother worked for the local sheriff's office, and he had agreed to help us with the aid of the police database.

Chapter Seven

The next evening, as I arrived home from work, the headlights of my Buick illuminated a figure skulking by the garage. Tate Richards was huddled beneath the overhang, trying to avoid the heavy downpour of rain that was flooding Sweet Water Bay.

"Hey, you okay?" I shouted, racing from the car toward the porch. Tate followed.

"I'm locked out of the house," he answered.

"Come on in, you're soaking wet."

Tate stepped inside, dropped his backpack, and discarded his drenched hoodie. He was saturated, and droplets of rain splashed rhythmically from the overgrown crop of hair that masked his face. I handed him a towel and directed him into the kitchen.

"Cool place."

"Thanks. Do you fancy a hot chocolate?"

Tate's eyes lit up, and a child's face looked back at me with the early stages of manhood evident around his chin and upper lip.

"Never too old for hot chocolate," I smiled.

With his hair dry and his lips planted firmly around the mug of warm chocolate, Tate seemed happy to chat.

"How come you're locked out; where are your parents?" I enquired.

"Dad's at work, and mom's taken Victoria to ballet class. They usually leave a spare under the mat, but I couldn't find it. She must've forgot."

"Well, you can wait here until someone gets home."

"I like your house; it feels friendly."

"It was my grandmother's; she left it to me when she passed. She was the friendliest person you would ever meet. I loved visiting her; I love this house."

Tate looked thoughtful, as if there was something on his mind, and he was deciding whether to share it or not. His cell beeped, and he explained, "Mom should be home in about twenty minutes."

"Okay, then time for another hot chocolate."

Connie and Roxy arrived home and joined us around the table. Tate's window of opportunity had disappeared.

When the lights of Marie's Range Rover turned into the driveway, Tate grabbed his belongings and headed for the door.

"Thanks for the drinks."

"Anytime, Tate, you're always welcome."

Tate nodded and disappeared into the heaviness of the rain. The car lights reversed, and they drove away.

Chapter Eight

That night, as the rain continued to batter Sweet Water, I tossed uneasily in bed. The spirit of the little boy still haunted my thoughts. His appearance was timely; he needed my help. I had hoped he might return, but so far, he hadn't.

Connie's sighting of the man in the top hat was no coincidence either. Were the two spirits connected, and if so, how?

By midnight, sleep had abandoned me completely, and I headed downstairs for a snack. Food was always a comfort when my mind was occupied; it helped me think more clearly and satisfied my unhappy digestive system.

I headed for the study. Standing in the darkness, I could just make out the names of the lost children on my recently acquired chalkboard. The light of a half-moon shone timidly through the window. In the shadow of its glow, I sensed someone standing beside me. The sudden icy touch of miniature fingers clasped my hand. I glanced down, but the child was gone. I knew it was him. The boy from the Richards' house. As I glanced back at the board, a finger of moonlight was illuminating a single name. That name was Jimmy Kale, the last child to disappear.

I sensed it was he who was trying to make contact. There was a deep sense of misery and isolation buried in his touch and a sadness so profound it defied explanation.

As morning broke, I found myself waking on the floor of the study, where I had spent the night hoping for Jimmy Kale to reappear. I longed to make contact with this child, but that wasn't usually something I instigated. The spirits found me, contacted me, showed me what they needed. I was going to need help from someone with more experience, and I knew just the person.

I called in sick that day and drove thirty miles towards Walrus Bay to visit with Sandy Brofsky. Sandy was my go-to person for all things weird. Author of several books on the paranormal, Sandy possessed her own special 'gifts,' and her knowledge of the spirit world was infinite. I desperately needed her help.

We had met by accident one balmy summer evening. I had felt the sting of a lone jellyfish as I paddled waist high in the ocean and tumbled onto the beach in dramatic fashion nursing a fiery swelling on my ankle. Sandy was sipping cocktails on the balcony of her coastal home and kindly rescued me. A bounty of alcoholic delights later and the throbbing pustule on my leg was forgotten, anaesthetized by Sandy's enthusiastic measure of shots. We became instant friends.

The outline of Sandy's stilted beach home came into view. Sandy was blessed with a magnificent ocean panorama and a healthy stretch of golden sand to call home. She was hanging from the balcony as I pulled in, and soon a beaming smile and a strong hug welcomed me.

"Oh, my goodness, Leni, look at you!" Sandy held me at arm's length and looked me up and down like a prize turnip. "Come in, come in. I'm so excited to see you. It's been way too long."

A pang of guilt fluttered at my conscience. Sandy was a dear friend with a huge heart, and I had never kept my promises to visit her.

"I'm sorry, Sandy. I'm a shit friend, I know."

"Nonsense, I know what it's like to be young and carefree. I want to hear everything."

Sandy was in her mid-sixties, with the body and mind of a teenager. She lived a simple existence, needing little from the modern world to make her happy. Her beach home, like her personality, was a cascade of vibrant colors. Driftwood furniture and an abundance of shells decorated the place in effortless style. She lived alone except for Bubba, her elderly, obese Persian feline. The beach house kept her grounded and, to some extent, safe from unnatural parameters. Keeping the mind clear and the body clean kept hostile spirits at bay.

Sandy mixed potent alcoholic concoctions to sip as we relaxed on the balcony. Crashing waves and seagulls were her only neighbors. The spritz of salty air carried by the evening breeze and the sight of an orange sun melting into the horizon completed the scene.

As cooler air replaced the warmth of the day, we retreated inside, dining on pasta and talking the hours away.

"So, you didn't drive all this way just for margaritas and pasta," declared Sandy. "I sense something is troubling you."

"You're right, of course. You're always right," I agreed as that pang of guilt hit me again.

"Oh, stop torturing yourself and spit it out," she demanded, ignoring the pitiful expression on my face.

"The spirit of a little boy has contacted me. He's a desperately tortured soul, and he needs my help, but I'm honestly not sure what I'm dealing with."

I drained the last of the delicious cocktail and suggested coffee may be more appropriate for the conversation we were about to embark on.

Sandy agreed and brewed a fresh pot as we sat by the glow of candlelight in her modest kitchen.

"The child is with you now," announced Sandy abruptly. "He's been here all night, standing in the shadows behind you. He's afraid, terrified. Something has him trapped in a world not between worlds, but somewhere..." Sandy gasped like it was her last breath. Terror held her rigid, her eyes growing wide as a tortuous grimace crept across her face.

"Sandy... Sandy, what's wrong?" I gripped her hand; the skin was cold and waxy beneath my fingers. I'd touched death before, and I knew how it felt.

"Oh, my God, Sandy," I shook her violently, but Sandy didn't respond. Sandy was dead.

How could this be? What had she seen that had frightened her to death in the middle of a sentence?

I didn't know what to do. My eyes stung with tears as I fought for clarity. I reached for my pocket. The cell wasn't there; it was sitting on the sofa in the living room just meters away. I tried to stand, but I was held in position, forced down by an unknown, unseen pressure. I was helpless in its power.

A strong wind whipped against the beach house, ripping through the shutters, extinguishing the candles. Darkness filled the room. I dared not to breathe as the contents of Sandy's home took flight around me.

Her statuesque figure was faintly visible as I fought for sight in the vastness of the night. My heart was jumping, gathering momentum, beating faster and faster. Then the room was still and silent once again.

The candles flickered to life spontaneously, and dancing flames lit the room.

The strength that held me in position had lifted, and I could move again.

I gazed around the room. The aftermath of destruction lay everywhere, scattered in the splintered fragments of Sandy's home.

I turned back towards my friend, except she wasn't there. Sandy had gone.

I was staring into the face of the man in the top hat.

I awoke to the sound of gulls. My head was heavy with confusion. It took a moment to recall my surroundings. Then, as I focused on the body of my friend sitting across from me, the whole evening came flooding back.

The color of death painted her skin in shades of decomposing gray. She was rigid and cold, her hands still resting on the table, her freshly painted fingernails of vibrant pink displayed. Her head had fallen forwards, blonde curls hiding her face.

I gently swept aside a lock of hair before releasing it immediately. The face it revealed was horrifying. Sandy's steel-blue eyes had been gouged from their sockets, her face ravaged by the blood loss that had followed. Her mouth was sown together pierced by thick, black twine that crossed back and forth between her lips. Sandy had suffered the same fate as Jimmy Kale.

Suddenly, the image of the man in the top hat flashed in front of me; he was the last thing I remembered about that fateful night. His shocking presence must have rendered me unconscious.

It was light outside; the sun was rising above a turbulent ocean as morning joggers picked up the pace through golden sand. The world was blissfully unaware of Sandy's demise, her grotesque disfigurement, and the existence of the man in the top hat.

I found my cell and dialed the local sheriff, but I did not wait to offer him an explanation. How could I rationally explain what he was about to find.

CHAPTER NINE

Sonia was making headway with contact details of the missing children. Her brother was helping. We met every Friday after work to discuss progress and add relevant information to the board in my study.

All but two children had known relatives living in the local area, making contact easy if necessary.

We arranged the children according to the date of their disappearance, beginning with Jenny Weaver, who was the first, and finishing with Jimmy Kale.

"Do you think we are looking for just one person?" Sonia questioned.

I thought for a while, "Good question, and I wish I knew the answer. All these children appear to have been abducted from within a five-mile radius of this town. Personally, I think we are looking for someone local, though there may be more than one person involved, but then I'm no profiler."

Sonia said nothing but stared at me as a wide grin crossed her lips.

"What?"

"You're no profiler, but I know someone who is," she teased, "my brother, Eric."

"Your brother, who works for the sheriff's office, and you never thought to mention that until now!"

Sonia nodded excitedly.

"I thought he was just a filing clerk; I had no idea he actually worked with the sheriff."

Sonia's revelation could be just the help we needed, and I urged her to contact Eric and arrange for him to visit the house.

Three days later, a tall, dark-haired, hazel-eyed stranger arrived on the front porch and introduced himself.

"Hey, I'm Eric, Sonia's brother," he declared.

I couldn't answer.

He was beguiling. My heart fluttered so fast I struggled to breathe, and my head felt so light I thought for a moment I might pass out. It was difficult to accept that the Adonis of a man who stood before me was the brother of the lovely, though somewhat plain-faced Sonia.

With a racing pulse and shaky legs, I invited him in.

I am not usually lost for words, but I found myself mumbling and stuttering in Eric's presence. I finally managed to offer him coffee by shaking the jar in front of him; no words needed.

Connie and Roxy appeared to save me further embarrassment, and the four of us sat around the kitchen table, waiting for Sonia to arrive.

The girls managed to chat to Eric with ease, while I sat staring at his every feature, memorizing every detail of his perfectly formed face. When he occasionally looked towards me, I broke his gaze by projecting my eyes down towards an empty coffee mug. When I dared to look back, he was immersed in conversation, though I sensed he knew I was watching him.

Eventually, Sonia burst into the room, spluttering apologies about a roadblock and detours. I nodded and smiled, hearing nothing of her explanation, as all my senses were focused on just one thing. Eric.

"Pull yourself together, girl," Roxy whispered in my ear. She had noticed my unusual silence and realized why.

I cleared my throat and pointed out the information we had so far, which in the scheme of things didn't seem like a whole lot.

I could feel Eric's piercing gaze as I tried desperately to focus, but the beads of sweat I felt beneath my linen shirt and the fiery sensation in both cheeks made me realize I was slowly having a meltdown.

Eric's solitary applause at the end of my speech was the final straw. My face resembled an overripe tomato, while dribbles of black mascara bled from the corner of each eye, and my usually well-tamed hair had frizzed uncontrollably in the humidity. I was a total wreck, and all because of a guy called Eric.

Noni would have loved this moment. She would have squeezed my flushed cheeks and teased me with broken Italian. She would have swooned over Eric and flirted like a woman half her age. Eric would have loved her back. Her zest for life was intoxicating. I missed her so much.

Eric seemed impressed by the library of children's names, ages, and dates we had previously collected. He cast a professional eye over the data, taking only minutes to deliver his assessment.

"I believe we are looking for a man of indeterminate age," he began.

"Why a man?" Roxy questioned.

"Men are by far the biggest perpetrators of crimes involving children, an unfortunate but well-known fact."

"So, we're looking for a pedophile?"

Connie's question echoed around the room.

"I'm not going to put that label on him at the moment," replied Eric. "Some men abduct children because they are vulnerable and powerless. It's all about control rather than sex."

Eric's words were disconcerting but valuable nonetheless.

"We must pray that these children didn't suffer at this man's hands," cried Sonia.

"I'm afraid we cannot make that assumption, Sonia, and realistically we may never know the answer," Eric continued. "Now, let's look at the dates. There appears to be no regular pattern: some years, two children were taken. In others, only one. We do know though that the abductions began in 1967 and suddenly stopped in 1977, a timeframe of ten years. Since then, there have been no more children reported missing, that we are aware of anyway."

"Which means what...?" Sonia interrupted.

"Which means that either our perpetrator died, stopped, which is highly unlikely, or is in prison."

"If he's in prison, then why are we wasting time looking for him," joked Roxy.

"He most probably went to prison for a different reason and not the abduction and probable murder of nineteen children," barked Eric, tensing at Roxy's visible amusement.

"Sorry," muttered Roxy, realizing her ill-timed conviviality had caused offence.

Eric nodded his acceptance, and the tension dispersed as he continued his analysis of the situation.

"The dates don't really help us unless we can determine a pattern, which isn't going to be easy. So, let's look at the children themselves, all relatively local and all between the ages of six and eight. Our abductor is very picky about age and area, which leads me to believe that he lives, or lived, somewhere in the neighborhood."

"So where do we go from here?" I finally mustered the courage to ask a question.

"Well, firstly, we need to check out the deaths of males from Sweet Water Bay and surrounding areas as far away as Frank's Town, Crowther's Beach, and Walrus Bay."

"I can do that," offered Sonia eagerly.

"Secondly, we need to find out who from those areas went to prison and why," Eric paused for a moment, "thinking about it, I can get that data at the sheriff's office."

"Okay, good start, but what can we do?" enquired Connie.

"I think you guys could find out the circumstances of each child's disappearance, for instance, time of day, where they were taken from. Hopefully some kind of pattern might emerge, which would be extremely useful."

Eric's own input had also been extremely useful, not to mention the fact that he'd turned the afternoon into a very pleasant visual experience. Connie put the kettle on while Roxy uncorked a bottle of vintage red.

The afternoon turned to evening, the wine was flowing, and conversation had turned to more amiable subjects.

Sonia went off to powder her nose.

The downstairs cloakroom was backing up and needed attention, so I pointed her in the direction of my bedroom, where she could use the attached bathroom.

"Where has my sister got to?" Eric slurred, examining his watch.

"You should never enquire what a lady is doing in the bathroom, Eric, but apparently she's gone to powder her nose," mused Roxy.

"Well, it is quite a big one," said Connie. Realizing her indiscretion, she quickly added, "The house I mean, not Sonia's nose."

"No, Connie, you were right the first time; Sonia's nose is rather on the large side, that's why it's taking so long to powder."

Everyone fell into uncontrollable, wine-induced laughter.

The grape was certainly bringing out Eric's mischievous side. His professional demeanor was enjoyable enough, but this side of Eric was positively sexy. I couldn't take my eyes off him and, if he were to admit it, he was feeling exactly the same.

Suddenly, all thoughts of romance dispersed as the kitchen fell into darkness. A distressed scream echoed through the house.

"Sonia," cried Eric.

I fumbled for a flashlight, but before I found it, the light was back, and Sonia came stumbling into the room.

Her face was ashen, her eyes magnified and staring wildly behind the lens of her glasses. Expelling incoherent words, she struggled to describe the reason for her anguish.

Roxy grabbed a whisky glass and filled it to the top, saying, "Here, drink this."

Sonia trembled as she forced the glass to her mouth and downed its contents.

"What's happened, Sonia?" demanded a concerned Eric, who had found the sight of his traumatized sister instantly sobering.

Sonia finally composed herself with the help of several refills, "I was upstairs in your room, just like you'd said. I was washing my hands when I heard a noise. I thought it was one of you guys, so I opened the bathroom door to find an old lady sitting on your bed. Her back was turned to me, so I couldn't see her face at first. I spoke to her like you'd taught me, Leni," Sonia downed another whisky as we waited for her to continue.

"Go on Sonia, you're doing great; what happened next?" I urged.

Sonia's eyes filled with tears as she battled to describe her encounter, "Then she turned to face me, but she was hideous; she had no eyes, and her mouth was sewn together. She reached out towards me as I ran for the bedroom door, and when I opened it, there was a little boy standing there with exactly the same horrible features. I was petrified. The lights went out, and I stumbled down the stairs as fast as I could... I think I've twisted my ankle."

I headed for the door. "Don't go up there, Leni," Sonia pleaded.

Roxy was at my shoulder, "Let's go. I'm right behind you."

We proceeded cautiously up the stairs in stealth formation. My bedroom door was slightly ajar, and I pushed it open slowly. The presence of an old woman in my bedroom was not concerning me, but her identity was. My first thought was of Noni, but she would not have appeared the way Sonia had described. My next thought was Cora Hempell recalling Chase Richards' words that night at the dinner party.

The room was empty now, with no sign of an old woman or a little boy. Roxy danced around the room, checking beneath the bed and in the closet.

"I think we can be pretty sure there's no one here now, Rox."

"Just making sure, Leni."

Eric decided it was time to take Sonia home and called a cab. Roxy consumed the contents of the last wine bottle and fell asleep on the kitchen table.

Connie followed me upstairs, so closely that I could feel her breath on my neck.

"Give a girl some space, Con," I moaned.

"Sorry, Leni, but that story has got me spooked; I'm not sure I can sleep alone tonight."

Connie was not the bed partner I had hoped for that evening. But in view of Sonia's strange encounter, I was more than happy for the company.

Even with a friend at my side, sleep ignored me, and I jumped at every noise. I had never felt unsafe or afraid at Noni's, but tonight was the exception.

Chapter Ten

The next morning, I awoke to the sound of Connie snoring. The bedroom was flooded with sunlight, and I stood at the window basking in its warmth. In the distance, I could hear voices shouting. It was coming from the direction of the Richards'. I leaned forward, my cheek pressing against the glass. The voices grew louder, and I recognized them now. Chase and Marie Richards were arguing on their driveway. I opened the window gently but too late. Chase had jumped into his car and sped off at high speed. Marie threw her hands in the air and disappeared into the house.

I wandered downstairs to find Roxy sprawled across the kitchen table, hair dyed red from the spillage of her wine glass. I woke her gently and coaxed her to bed.

Waiting patiently for the coffee to brew, my thoughts turned to Eric, Sonia's frightening encounter in my bedroom, and the mental promise I made to myself never to share a bed with Connie again.

It wasn't the sound of bubbling Kenyan beans that shattered my thoughts but a desperate banging at the side door. I could see through the glass panel that Tate Richards was the culprit.

"Steady on there, you'll put the glass through," I joked, letting Tate into the kitchen. "Are you feeling okay, buddy; it's only half past ten on a Sunday morning. Are you sleepwalking or something?"

Tate was not laughing. His face was serious, his eyes watery, and he almost bowled me over as he rushed through the door.

"Hey, what's going on? Are you okay?" I queried, concerned.

Tate sat staring at me for a moment, fighting back the tears, saying nothing.

I poured two cups of strong coffee and sat beside him, waiting patiently for his reply. "I can't live in that house any longer," he blubbed.

I placed a reassuring hand on his shoulder, "Parents can be like that. I heard them this morning in the driveway."

Tate looked blank, "It's not them. I mean it is them, but it's that house."

"Has something happened?" I asked, my thoughts rewinding to that first meeting with Jimmy Kale in the Richards' dining room.

"Something's always happening, ever since we moved in. I just hate it there," Tate sobbed.

I waited for him to collect himself, wondering if his distraught state was the result of encounters with the man in the top hat or the little boy whose spirit resided there.

"Here, drink this. You can talk to me, you know, if you want to."

Tate sipped at the china mug. I'd laced it with rum. Noni's old remedy: good strong coffee with a healthy tot of Old Jamaican, her cure for everything.

Tate seemed calmer with each sip. Noni was right.

"There's more where that came from," I joked. Tate smiled and wiped the remnant of a tear from his cheek.

"You ready to tell me what's going on?"

Tate lowered his head and fumbled with his fingers.

"What did you mean when you said, 'it's that house'?"

Tate continued to stare at his hands, "You're gonna think I'm crazy, Leni, but I'm not imagining things."

"Nothing wrong with a little crazy, I mean look at Roxy and Connie, they don't come much crazier."

Tate sniggered.

"Everyone has changed since we came to live here. It's the house, there's something not right. I can feel it. Does that make any sense?"

"Perfect sense. Old houses can be dressed for the twenty-first century, but the history still remains. A couple of hundred years of different people walking the halls, climbing the stairs, experiencing happy times and sad ones too are all imprinted within its walls. Even though you've changed its appearance, you can't change its feel."

"I suppose you're right, but can a house change the people who live in it?"

I thought for a moment, searching for a comforting reply, "Of course, your parents took on a lot when they bought that house. They moved area, you and Victoria moved schools, the bills will be bigger. Worry alone can change people."

"I really don't think they have worries though; they are like different people, Leni. My parents and my sister feel like strangers to me."

"Okay, so describe them to me. What's changed?"

Tate was pensive, "Dad hardly ever comes home. He sleeps at the hospital most nights, and when he does come home, they argue. When dad texts to say he's not coming home, mom drinks. She drinks a lot. She misses appointments, even forgets to pick up Victoria from school sometimes."

Tate's words were worrying. I fought for a rational explanation. Was Chase having an affair, had Marie found out and was consoling herself with alcohol, or was she simply depressed. Whatever the reason, something was keeping Chase away from home and making Marie very unhappy. Tate's portrait painted a very different picture from the one I had witnessed a couple of months earlier. "You know, Tate, sometimes parents go through these phases. I suspect your dad's just really busy at work. That's why your mom's drinking, because she misses him. I really wouldn't worry too much."

Tate considered my reply, "I get that, Leni, and you're probably right, but then there's Victoria."

A chill coasted my spine at the mention of her name.

"What's wrong with your sister?" I hesitated to ask, fearing Tate's reply.

"Well, for starters, she talks to herself," he began.

"Oh, that's pretty normal. You can ask my mom about Pookie bear," I chuckled, trying to make light of the situation, "children sometimes make up imaginary friends…"

"Yeah, maybe, but did you speak to yours in a different language?"

There went that chill again. I searched for a plausible answer.

"Well, no, but make-believe friends speaking make-believe languages only they understand isn't unusual at Victoria's age."

Tate wasn't buying it. He took out his cell and placed it on the table, "Listen to this—I've recorded her."

Victoria's sweet tones could clearly be heard. The language she spoke was certainly not recognizable, though whatever it was, she spoke it fluently.

I struggled to hide my surprise at the voice of five-year-old Victoria Richards conversing so eloquently.

"See what I mean?" queried Tate.

I did see exactly what he meant, but at the same time, I wasn't about to send the teenager away feeling worse than when he arrived. I pondered an appropriate response.

"I think… you have a very talented little sister."

"You recognize the language?" questioned Tate.

"No, I don't, and it's really no surprise, because your sister is talking gobbledygook. No-one would understand it. It's a make-believe language that only children and their toys understand."

Tate shrugged. He didn't really seem to buy my explanation, but he pretended to accept it.

"Look, if you're worried, send me a copy of that recording. I'll get a friend to check it out."

Tate said nothing, but the ping of my cell indicated he had already sent it.

I began to prepare pancakes in a bid to change Tate's train of thought, but even the aroma of maple syrup and bacon wasn't enough to distract him.

"She has all her meals in her room," he stated between finishing the last morsel from his stack of six.

"Well, that's a little antisocial, I admit, but there's been a lot of changes in your lives recently, maybe she just feels safer and more secure in her bedroom." I replied.

There was silence for a moment. I prayed I had answered Tate's questions successfully, but then...

"There's always a light on in her bedroom at night; don't you think that's odd?"

"Not really. I always slept with a night light. Kids can be scared of the dark."

"This isn't a night light; it's the ceiling light," Tate continued.

That is a bit odd, I thought.

"Doesn't your mom turn it off?"

"That's the thing: she does, but then it comes back on again."

"She probably turns it off when Victoria's gone to sleep," I proffered.

"Well, it's always on in the early hours when I get up for juice, and the other thing is... I think there's someone in there with her."

That line was the stinger. Chills coursed the entirety of my body. My thoughts turned to Connie's description of the man in the top hat standing at the little girl's window.

"You know, Tate, imagination is always heightened when we're tired or thirsty, especially in the middle of the night when our mind likes to play tricks on us. I'm sure whatever you think is going on with Victoria has a perfectly rational explanation."

I crossed my fingers, hoping Tate would accept my words and drop the subject. The offer of extra pancakes did the trick.

He hovered beside the stove, and I satisfied his appetite with a second stack.

As the afternoon sun was hovering over the backyard, Tate was ready to head home.

"Thanks, Leni," he shouted, "same time next Sunday?"

"Anytime, Tate," I shouted back as he disappeared from view. That conversation left me uneasy.

Boys of Tate's age were usually shallow, immersed in video games, lost in music, and desperately self-centered.

For a teenager to notice such changes in his environment, they must be pretty significant.

Chapter Eleven

Sonia was unwilling to visit the house following her encounter with the disfigured spirits, so we met in the local coffee shop downtown. She had some findings to discuss and was eager to share.

Part of me was hoping Eric had accompanied her, but only Sonia was occupying a window booth when I arrived.

"I've ordered," she announced as I took a seat opposite her.

"Great, so what's going on?"

Sonia pulled a file of paper from her satchel and placed it in front of me.

"These are the names of every man who died in the area in 1977," she exclaimed excitedly, "there's quite a few."

"I see," I responded, flicking through the pages quickly.

"I've crossed out the ones who died after February 4th, 1977."

"Okay, so that leaves how many?"

"Fifty-seven. That's not so bad, is it?"

Not wanting to burst Sonia's bubble of excitement, I smiled and shook my head. I was hoping the numbers were a lot lower.

"We just need to match this up with Eric's list because some of these died in prison, apparently."

My heart missed a beat at the sound of Eric's name and the possibility that he might make an appearance after all.

"So, when are you planning on us getting together with Eric?" I queried as a rush of excitement coursed through my body.

"Well, he's away for the weekend, so will have to be next week sometime, whenever you're free."

The sentence was thought-provoking; Eric being away for the weekend was not something I wanted to hear. Who was he away with? Did he have a girlfriend? The thought was unbearable, and I couldn't bring myself to explore it any further.

"I'm free whenever you and Eric are; just let me know."

Sonia nodded and drained her latte. She followed me to the door and headed in the direction of the library.

The following week, I met Sonia at an unknown address on the other side of Sweet Water Bay, a town called Harbor Cove.

It was set beside a coastal inlet and had a population of around thirty. I followed the GPS to a duplex property hidden within lush gardens and boasting a communal pool and tennis court. The rear of the complex sat yards from the ocean. It was a charming place, quaint and unspoiled.

I soon realized I had arrived at Eric's home. I approached the stairway to the upper balcony just as Eric was returning from an early evening swim. Curls of tousled, wet hair framed his tanned face. Wearing nothing but swim shorts and a perfect smile, he met me at the bottom of the steps. "Hey, Leni, come on up, follow me," he exclaimed with a blinding flash of flawless teeth.

His sculpted torso and muscular legs climbed the stairs in front of me. How I made it to the top was a miracle, my legs weakened at the sight of Eric's masculinity saved only by the rush of adrenaline that his presence induced.

Eric disappeared to change, leaving me on the balcony with a spritzer.

I had almost forgotten the reason for my visit, mesmerized by the sound of the ocean and the shimmering horizon beyond.

Moments later, Sonia arrived, and I remembered.

The three of us huddled around a marble dining table where Sonia painstakingly read each name from her list, as Eric and I searched for matches on his and crossed them off appropriately.

His aroma was intoxicating, and I found it increasingly hard to concentrate.

Two hours later, our list of fifty-seven had reduced, and by midnight, we had twenty-three names left. It was crazy to think that one of them could be our suspect. As Sonia hinted it was time to say goodnight, I asked to use the bathroom. I used the opportunity to go scanning the house for pictures of an adoring Eric wrapped in the arms of a zero-sized leggy blond. Thankfully, there were none. When I emerged, Sonia had already left. Eric was lounging amidst a cascade of sumptuous cushions on the sofa nearest to his lively fireplace, neat whisky in his hand. He posed as if he were a model on the cover of a glossy magazine, displaying a stylish home around him. Eric had most definitely chosen the wrong career.

"Well, goodnight, Eric, thanks for the drinks."

"My pleasure, Leni. You okay to drive?"

"I'm pretty sure so," I replied, immediately regretting the words as I heard them leave my mouth. I wanted to retract that statement and spend the night in Eric's luxury abode. A silent scream pierced my core as I hurried towards the staircase, scolding my naivety as I descended into the darkness outside.

"Goodnight then, drive safely," I heard him call in the distance.

The avenue seemed darker than usual as I swung into the driveway, unaware of a small figure lurking in the shadows.

Suddenly, a child flashed in the headlights, and I swerved hard, braking to an abrupt stop. I raced from the car, expecting to find a lifeless body in front of it. There was nothing to see: no child, no one. The street was empty except for a ginger tabby straddling the fence line.

I gathered myself together and pulled the car safely into position. My heart was pounding so hard I could feel it inside my head. Reaching the porch, I dropped the house key in my haste to enter. The porch light did not illuminate; the bulb had been removed, and my cell battery was dead. I fumbled in the darkness, searching for the missing key.

My fingers found an object, smooth and rounded, a cane perhaps; definitely not the elusive key. I explored curiously, sliding my hand upwards. The shape of the smoothness changed, and I felt something cold and waxy beneath my grip. A hand. I gazed upwards as the face of the man in the top hat stared back at me. I hit the ground hard.

I awoke on the sofa to the concerned faces of my friends.

"Oh, thank God! You okay?" asked a worried Roxy.

I stared into oblivion, focusing on the living room clock: 3 am, where had I been since midnight? Then I remembered.

I sat bolt upright as the images flooded back. I wished they hadn't. The slender, smooth surface of the cane in my hand. The slow upward movement as I followed its line in the darkness. It was his, the man in the top hat. I shook myself violently trying to rid him from my thoughts. The emptiness of his eyes, the white painted face worn like a death mask, and the crisscross pattern traversing his lips flashed into view. It wasn't his outward appearance that sent a tsunami of fear crashing over me, but rather the feeling of agonizing desolation that raged inside him. The touch of our hands, revealing a snapshot of the misery and degradation he represented, innocent children sacrificed and mutilated by his hand. I could hardly dare to remember the pain of their screams and the torment on their faces. Death was their only release.

He was everything that was evil.

"Leni, you're worrying me now. Speak to me, please," Connie shook the torment from my thoughts and covered my shivers with blankets.

I lay back on the sofa, gripping Connie's hand in mine. "I think I met the Devil!"

Chapter Twelve

My midnight encounter with the man in the top hat was permanently etched within my thoughts, spreading like a deadly virus; it consumed every waking moment and interrupted any hope of sleep.

I never recounted my experience, saving my friends from the horrific details, and aside from my terrified admission to Connie, I denied any knowledge of having met the devil. The less they knew about the man in the top hat, the better. It was the only way to keep them safe.

I was desperate to discover the truth behind the missing children and reveal the identity of their executioner. Twenty-three suspects stalked the list of possibilities, and the investigation began. Three suspects were dementia patients who, having contracted the degenerative disease at an early age, were highly improbable candidates.

Two suspects were Catholic priests, which did not eliminate them entirely, though the penchant for children amongst the clergy was more of a sexual than murderous nature. A further three men had been involved in life-changing accidents occurring during the timeline, but as the abductions had continued following their tragedies, it seemed sensible to remove them from the list. One man had transitioned and relocated to Arizona.

Fourteen possibilities remained.

I tapped their names into social media platforms, trawling through posts and photographs, relatives and friends, searching for signs of murderous intent. Disappointingly, the majority were living mundane lives with children of their own, revealing no signs of a double life involving abduction.

The two remaining names were Barclay Thomas and Erasmus Cobb. Neither man held a social profile, living as shadows amongst the local community. I was drawn to them, and I was eager to find out why.

Barclay Thomas appeared familiar. It transpired he was a kindergarten teacher at the school Victoria now attended.

Barclay, aged 56, was unmarried with no children. His social life appeared limited, and he had lived with his mother until her demise five years earlier. Barclay Thomas was currently top of my suspect list.

I decided to take a couple of days' annual leave and give my suspect the attention he deserved. Sonia was keen to accompany me, and we sat like wannabe detectives outside Crowther's Bay Elementary, desperate for a sighting of the man himself.

As Barclay Thomas left school that afternoon, he jumped into an aging Corvette, with Sonia and I hot on his tail.

"Gosh! This is exciting, Leni."

Sonia was pumped with emotion, a side of her I had never seen before.

We followed the unsuspecting Mr Thomas to the gas station, where he fueled up and shopped.

He swung into the parking lot of Breakers Bar and disappeared inside.

"Should we follow him?" queried Sonia.

"I'm not sure. Let's sit a while and wait. If he doesn't come back out in twenty, we'll go in."

Twenty minutes with Sonia was painful. She could not sit still. "Hell, Sonia, you'd never make a detective. You're too eager," I declared.

Sonia looked dejected, "I'm just excited, that's all."

"Okay, girl, let's haul your excited ass inside, but follow my lead; don't go making it obvious why we're there."

Sonia gladly agreed, and we headed inside.

The place was dingy; dull lighting and dark furniture made it that way. Only the bar area, lit like a Christmas tree, was instantly visible.

We perched on a couple of stools at one end, a good vantage point from where we could see customers coming and going.

"What can I get you, ladies?" The question came from a thin, red-haired boy in denim overalls who looked too young to be working, let alone serving behind the bar.

"Two spritzers, please."

"Coming right up," he replied confidently.

The bar was relatively empty, save for a couple of elderly men drinking beers at the opposite end.

There were a couple of booths by the window and a pool table in the middle of the room accompanied by an old-style Wurlitzer playing country tunes.

"Seems pretty quiet tonight?" I stated, engaging the bartender in conversation.

"Yeah, that's for sure, but it'll liven up later on. Always does."

"You've worked here a while, then?"

"Sure have, my pa owns it, live upstairs, can't get away from the place."

"You must make a lot of friends in your line of work? Regulars, I mean."

"Oh, sure, we get regulars, not really friends though, just fellas needing a drink after work or old timers with nothing much else to do." He nodded towards the two guys drinking beers, perched like two parrots deep in conversation at the other end of the bar, then added, "You're new though, haven't seen you in here before."

"No, we were supposed to meet someone, but they've stood us up."

"That's a shame... excuse me, ladies, I have a customer," the boy headed off towards a man standing just a few yards away. Close enough to hear the bartender ask, "Same again, Barclay?"

Sonia squeezed my arm.

"Stay calm," I commanded.

Barclay Thomas was of average height and average weight, a nondescript, solemn-looking man. His hairline was receding, and that which remained had turned a peppery gray. He sported black-framed glasses and an unruly mustache. He spoke with a southern drawl as he thanked the bartender for the double shot and wandered into the corner of the room, where he sat hidden in the shadows, drinking alone.

We finished our drinks and headed back to the car. There, we waited for Barclay Thomas to emerge. It was a couple of hours later that his lonely figure stepped into the moonlight. He staggered across the car park in search of his car, stopping briefly to attempt to unlock a car that wasn't his. Barclay Thomas was intoxicated. I seized the opportunity, jumping from the car before Sonia had noticed that I'd gone.

"Hey, mister, you okay?" I headed towards him, "You can't drive a car in that state; you're a liability."

"You a cop?" he demanded.

"No."

"You sound like a cop."

"I'm just a concerned citizen."

"Concerned... concerned about what?" His speech was slurred as he muttered incoherently. He staggered from one car to the next, refusing to accept his inebriated state.

"I'm concerned that you're gonna try driving a car while under the influence, and if you continue, then I'll have to call the cops."

"Do what you want. I don't care," he mumbled.

"You will when they haul your ass into a cell for the night. Let me call you a cab."

For a moment, he stopped what he was doing and turned to look at me.

"Lady, they'll haul my ass whether I'm drunk or not. They don't need an excuse."

Barclay's words struck a chord. He'd obviously had encounters with the local police before, and I needed to keep him talking to see what I could find out.

"They can't do that; you must have done something wrong."

Barclay spat as the bourbon-induced words burst from his lips, "Just being me is wrong to them."

"I'm sorry, I don't follow what you mean?"

"I'm a man, I live alone, I've never married, got no children. Therefore, I must be gay or a pedophile!"

Barclay was beginning to tire. He clung to the back of a rusty old truck, his legs buckling beneath him.

"Well, are you?" I pushed for the answer, but the red-haired bartender was beside me, steadying Barclay as he directed him back towards the bar.

"I've got this, thanks. I'll call him a cab." The bartender disappeared with Barclay clinging to his arm.

I headed back to the car, where Sonia was desperate for information.

"I was so close to getting him to talk, Sonia."

"What shall we do now then?"

"Let's see how he gets home and where he lives; then we can ask Eric to check him out for us."

Sonia nodded. Within minutes, headlights lit the parking lot.

"Here we go, Sonia, hold on."

I swung the car out behind the taxi that Barclay Thomas had just been bundled into. It led us along the interstate and turned off towards Frank's Town. We stopped a short distance from where Barclay exited the taxi with the help of the driver, who seemed to know him. The two men disappeared inside a small two-story house, lights on, lights off, the thud of a door closing. Minutes later, the taxi drove away.

"What do we do now?" asked Sonia.

"We wait a few minutes, make sure he's passed out, and then we can take a closer look."

"Oh, Leni, I haven't felt this excited since... well, I don't know when." Sonia's voice pitched higher the more excited she became.

"Keep it down, Sonia, let's not draw attention to ourselves." I scanned the street for spectators. All seemed quiet, no twitchy curtains or insomniacs to report.

"Okay, follow me, close the door quietly; don't slam it, we don't want to wake the neighbors."

Sonia followed my instructions perfectly, and we headed across the street to Barclay's shabby-looking house. The front garden was heavily neglected, overgrown by weeds and long grass. The porch was collapsing, a crumbling framework of rotten wood framed an equally decaying front door. The driveway was a graveyard of discarded furniture and appliances. Even the dimness of the streetlights couldn't mask the shabbiness of Barclay Thomas's home.

We picked our way steadily to the back of the property, knee high in garbage bags. Dogs barked in the distance, but no sound came from inside Barclay's house.

I tried the backdoor, locked. Windows, also locked. Then, I spotted a basement window, slightly ajar.

"You stay here and hold open the window, keep a look out and let me know if you hear or see anyone," I told Sonia.

"I'll go inside and take a look around." My instructions were clear, and Sonia nodded her understanding.

I slipped through the opening, completely missing the ledge I had found with my foot, and landed with a thud on the basement floor.

Sonia's face appeared beneath the window. I told her, "I'm okay, slipped that's all."

The basement smelled damp and musty, a theme I considered would run throughout the house.

The light of my cell phone searched the darkness. A wooden staircase led upwards to an unlocked door and out into Barclay Thomas's kitchen.

'Squalid' would be the most accurate description of Barclay's home. The kitchen stank of rotten food, dirty pots and excessive amounts of rubbish spewed across the floor. The living room wasn't any better. There was the definition of a sofa hidden beneath piles of books, magazines and paper. A small, old-fashioned television sat in one corner, its only companion a large coffee table littered with empty bottles and glasses.

It was evident that Barclay Thomas had a drink problem. I rifled through the papers and magazines, no pornographic images, just mounds of fishing monthlies and piles of invoices.

It was the weirdest feeling sneaking around someone else's house without their knowledge, but it was the only way I could gain an insight into the man who had become my main suspect. I ventured to the bottom of the stairs and looked up. All seemed quiet; no lights glowed, no sounds.

I stepped carefully, each tread creaking beneath my feet, listening intently for movement.

My breath was noisy in the silence. I stopped momentarily at the top of the stairs, assessing the doors in front of me. Three doors, one left, one right and one straight ahead. I moved slowly towards the first. I didn't need to enter; the odor seeping from within signified this was the bathroom. I passed quickly, holding my nose, and headed to the door at the end of the landing. This was a bedroom, presumably his mother's, judging by the decor. Stranded in an era when chintz and lace were fashionable, the room was at least forty years out of date. It was relatively neat though, untouched by magazines, and I suspected Barclay never visited.

I hesitated beside the third door. A low rumble emanated from inside, and I realized Barclay was snoring. I gripped the handle and turned as quietly and slowly as possible. It opened to reveal Barclay Thomas prostrate on a quilted bedspread.

A sliver of moonlight through the drapes made it possible to see that the room was sparse. A wooden rocking chair by the window and a chest of drawers beside the bed. I pulled at the top drawer carefully, opening it just enough to fit my hand inside. Feeling around, I caught the pages of a book. It revealed itself to be a diary. I left the room hastily with the treasure in my pocket, knowing there was a lot to be learnt from the pages of a person's daily scribbles.

"You've been an age, was just debating whether to come after you," scolded Sonia as I emerged through the basement window.

"Sorry, not something you can rush, had to be careful not to wake him."

"Well, find anything?"

"Just this," I held the prize diary in the air, "couldn't read it in there, wasn't enough light, so I've borrowed it."

"'Borrowed it,' sounds like you mean to give it back?"

"Depends what we find inside. Come on, let's go home and read it."

Chapter Thirteen

Sonia reluctantly agreed to sit in the kitchen while we pored over the contents of Barclay Thomas's diary, but before we could even turn the first page, there was a frantic knock at the front door. Marie Richards was standing on the porch in her nightclothes, with Victoria huddled beside her. She was heavily distressed, almost hysterical. She pushed Victoria towards me, begging, "Please, can you look after her for me?"

Victoria's eyes were pooled with tears; she looked as if she had been plucked from her sleep and dragged into the night. I comforted her, holding her close, cradling her tiny body against my own. "Of course, Marie, but what's going on? Is everything okay?"

Marie's bottom lip trembled as she mouthed, "Chase has got a gun, and he's threatening to use it."

I rushed Victoria inside and mounted her on Sonia's knee, saying, "Look after her for me; I think the Richards need help." Before Sonia could reply, I was gone, running into the night, chasing behind the distraught Marie.

I lost sight of her as I reached the steps of the Richards' beautiful home, but the door was ajar. The front of the house was cloaked in darkness, and no sounds could be heard. I stepped cautiously inside. I dare not call out for fear of Chase mistaking me for the police and doing something stupid, so I stepped as stealthily as possible as I crossed the living room towards the staircase.

The house looked different in the dark, felt different, even smelled different. There was a faint repugnant odor that grew stronger as I ventured further. The flowers on the dining room table were dead, and in the fruit bowl beside them sat an array of decaying apples.

At the top of the staircase was a faint glimmer of light and the muted sound of voices. I ascended quickly and quietly, the voices growing louder as I reached the top. I waited, listening outside the master bedroom. Marie's trembling words were repetitive, "Chase, please put the gun down."

I sensed Chase was standing beside the bed, as I couldn't see him through the crack of the door. Marie was clearly visible on the other side of the room. Tate was standing directly behind the door, and I could hear his breathing, erratic and shallow.

Chase was crying and mumbling, his voice shaking with emotion. Tate was crying now, and Marie was pleading.

I had two choices: leave and call 911, if a neighbor hadn't already, or barge into the room, knocking Tate out of harm's way in a bid to wrestle Chase to the ground and disarm him.

There wasn't time to wait. Chase sounded too unstable, and I needed to act now. Without a second thought, I shoved at the door as hard as I could, toppling Tate to the ground, and raced across the bedroom towards a startled Chase. I grabbed his arm; my target was the gun. He fought back, and the gun fired. We fell to the ground, tumbling together in a moment of chaos. Then there was calm.

I hurried to my feet, searching for the gun. Chase had lost his grip on it as I wrestled for control. There, by the cabinet, lay the small, silver firearm resting in the thickness of the rug. I emptied the chamber and placed it on the bed.

Tate was on his feet now, eyes wide with fear as he realized Marie was not moving.

"Mom," he cried, rushing to her lifeless body.

Chase, fearing he had killed his wife, tucked himself into a ball and began to sob uncontrollably.

"Move, Tate, let me see," I barked.

Marie was unconscious, but she wasn't dead. Blood was seeping from her shoulder where the stray bullet had pierced.

"She'll be okay; she has a shoulder wound, nothing serious," I soothed.

"Why isn't she moving?" Tate cried.

"She hit her head, Tate, and knocked herself out. She will be fine."

As Tate cradled his mother in his arms, I returned to check on Chase, who was still locked in the fetal position.

This was not the man I had met months earlier; this was a shocking, almost unrecognizable shadow of him. His vibrant curls were lackluster gray, dark circles framed frightened, vacant eyes, and his normally sun-kissed skin was ashen. Chase Richards had aged beyond explanation.

I crouched beside him, "The police are here," I whispered. Chase didn't respond. His eyes remained fixed and staring.

"If there's anything you want to say, Chase, do it now," I pleaded for him to explain, but all Chase Richards repeated as he left the house in handcuffs was "I didn't want to hurt her. I didn't want to hurt her."

As the patrol cars dispersed and the ambulance ferried Marie to the hospital, I guided Tate in the direction of Noni's.

Sonia was asleep on the sofa, Victoria nestled beside her wrapped in my grandmother's knitted shawl.

I nudged Sonia gently. She opened her eyes and asked, "Everything okay?"

"It wasn't, but it will be," I reassured.

Tate moved his sleeping sister from the couch, and they spent what was left of that night in the guest bedroom together. I had so many questions for Tate Richards, but they would have to wait. We all needed sleep.

Chapter Fourteen

The following morning, I drove Tate and Victoria to the hospital to visit their mom.

She was drowsy and had lost a lot of blood, but removal of the bullet had been successful, and it was a possibility that she would be discharged in the next couple of days.

On the way home, we stopped at the Richards' house to pick up spare clothes and supplies.

The pungent odor that had attacked my senses the night before lingered, now even stronger.

Even bathed in the midday sunshine, the house felt cold, barren, and dramatically different from the one I had experienced a few months earlier. The warmth of the family that had brought it back to life was gone. The brightness of its contemporary rooms and neutral decor was lost, overshadowed by the abyss of darkness that corrupted it. There was a presence, something strong, something wicked that had taken up residence, and it frightened me.

I hurried Victoria up the stairs towards her bedroom. It was here the smell was strongest. I fought against the window, but it wouldn't move.

"That doesn't open," exclaimed Victoria as she saw me battling.

"Since when?"

"Since just after we moved in."

Victoria hummed happily as she filled a pink, sparkly backpack with her favorite possessions.

"Okay, meet me downstairs in ten. There's ice cream waiting for you at my place!"

I found Tate sitting on his bed. His backpack was still empty.

"Hey, couldn't decide what to pack?" I joked.

"What's gonna happen to dad now?" he asked thoughtfully.

"Well, I can't say for sure, but he will be assessed and probably appear in court."

"Assessed for what? Will he go to prison? He didn't mean to hurt mom. He didn't know what he was doing. What..."

Tate was visibly distraught by the happenings of the previous night. Truth is, I didn't really know what would happen.

"Look, your mom will be home from the hospital in a couple of days. She will explain to the police that what happened was an accident, and I'm pretty sure everything will go back to normal."

"Normal?" Tate turned to look at me, "Things haven't been normal since we moved in. It's this house; I told you there's something here. It made dad go crazy."

Even though I suspected that the malevolence inhabiting the Richards' home was probably responsible for Chase's actions, I wasn't prepared to admit that to Tate.

"Let's get you out of here for a couple of days. Pack your bag and meet me downstairs."

I perched on the steps just outside the front door. Waiting inside made me uneasy. The Richards' house was disturbing, and whatever they were dealing with wasn't just going to go away. I now understood what Tate had meant that Sunday morning when he visited me teary and distressed.

Whatever had taken up residence would require expert help and, thankfully, I knew just the man for the job.

Chapter Fifteen

Connie and Roxy fussed over our young guests and planned a picnic at the beach. They disappeared early the next morning with Victoria, while Tate chose to lounge in bed.

Sonia was on her way over. We still needed to go through Barclay Thomas's diary, and today was as good a day as any, with almost everyone being out of the house.

At first, there was nothing much of interest to feed our enthusiasm, but then the entries took a surprising turn.

Barclay often talked about his father and the couple who had moved into the house next door.

On further reading, it became apparent that the couple were none other than Cora and Baxter Hempell.

"Must have been their first house, before they bought the house here next to Noni," I exclaimed.

"Makes sense," agreed Sonia, "Frank's Town is much smaller than Sweet Water, a mixed-race couple probably wasn't so obvious living there."

"I think a mixed-race couple in the sixties would be obvious anywhere Sonia, even Frank's Town."

We turned the page. The entry on the 26th of January, 1967, reported the disappearance of Byron Hempell. Barclay wrote:

> *"Father told me today that Byron Hempell was missing. He is around my age, maybe a little older. I often saw him looking out of his bedroom window. He waved at me. He looked sad. He never came out to play, so we never met in person.*
>
> *Frankie from school says it's because he's a vampire, and if he walks into the daylight he will burn, but I don't think I believe him."*

A couple of days later, Barclay writes:

> *"I heard father talking about Byron Hempell today, telling granny when we visited her after church. He said he thought Byron's father was involved and the cops did too, but they couldn't prove it."*

It was no secret that Baxter Hempell was the first suspect interrogated by the local police over his missing child. Family members are always the first to be eliminated, and Baxter was eventually released without charge. Presumably, there was little or no evidence to substantiate his involvement.

Sonia continued to peruse the diary whilst I brewed coffee. We chatted jovially, joking and giggling, and then suddenly, the room fell silent.

I turned to find Sonia face down in the open diary.

"Sonia, you okay?"

Sonia didn't reply at first, but then...

She lifted her head to face me. Her beautiful green eyes had turned a milky white. Her mouth was open as though she was about to speak, and yet she said nothing. I approached her cautiously, too late, and she grabbed my arm and pulled my face to within inches of hers. Her mouth still open, dribbling saliva, she bellowed, "SHE'S GOING TO DIE."

The voice did not belong to Sonia. It was indescribable, paralyzing, evil.

Sonia's head hit the table with a thud and shocked her into the realization that something had just occurred, though she remembered nothing.

I settled my nerves with mugs of hot, strong coffee as Sonia nursed the growing bruise across her forehead and the headache that was accompanying it. I didn't scare easily, but Sonia's performance had certainly changed that. The voice that spoke was so diabolical it was not going to be easy to forget, and the words even more so. Who was going to die?

I thought back to the night of my meeting with the man in the top hat. I thought of Tate's description of his home and family, and the transformation of Chase Richards. I knew that whatever had momentarily possessed Sonia was the same evil that lurked in the Richards' home. I knew we hadn't seen or heard the last of it; it was gathering momentum, growing stronger. I knew there was a war coming.

Three mugs of sugary coffee for me and two Tylenol for Sonia, and we continued to peruse Barclay Thomas's diary.

Pages of routine, everyday activities repeated, hardly worth recording in a diary at all. A morsel of a fantasy about a girl called Sherri, a tad more interesting, and then this:

> *"Egan never came to school today. I missed him. I had no one to talk to at lunchtime. Egan's my best friend."*

Sadly, Egan Reed never made it to school ever again, as Barclay later describes his disappearance:

> *"Egan was stolen from his bed last night. No one knows what happened; he's just disappeared. He's the fourth kid to go missing. Sometimes, I'm scared in case I get taken.*
>
> *Frankie says it only happens at night because it's a vampire that takes the kids, and it lives with the Hempells."*

On our list of missing children, we found the names of Egan Reed, Ruby Kline, and Jenny Weaver, the first three to have disappeared.

It was time to return Barclay Thomas's diary and have a chat with him.

When the gang returned from the beach, I said nothing of the unnerving voice that had borrowed Sonia's larynx earlier in the day. Tate had never left the bedroom. I was the only witness.

Chapter Sixteen

When Barclay Thomas arrived home from work the following day, I was sitting on the steps of his porch holding the diary.

"Who are you? If you're selling something, I'm not interested," he grumbled.

"Not selling, returning." I held the diary in front of him.

He grabbed it from my hand, examining it carefully. "How did you get this?" Barclay glanced towards his open front door. "You broke in. I'm calling the police."

"No need, I've already called them." Barclay looked confused, and I continued, "You had a break-in, but it wasn't me. I saw someone running from the house, and they dropped this. I picked it up and dialed 911. I figured you might want it back along with an explanation, so I've been waiting for you."

Barclay's demeanor softened, "Oh, I see. I'm sorry I accused you."

"No problem; I was driving by and saw him, hope there's nothing else missing."

Barclay hurried past me and disappeared inside the grubby dwelling. I waited for him to return, knowing that nothing had been touched, just the lock on the front door had been damaged. I needed my story to have credibility.

"There's nothing missing, thank you again," said Barclay gratefully after reappearing in the doorway.

"Hey, don't you work at the elementary school?" I questioned as Barclay began to retreat.

Barclay stepped forward, his face in full view, "Err, yes, yes I do," he hesitated.

"I thought so. My neighbors' kid goes there: Victoria Richards."

Barclay nodded at the mention of the name and lingered for a moment before retreating again.

I had to think quickly; I needed him to engage in conversation, not close the door in my face.

"D'you fancy a drink?" I uttered cautiously, "There's a Starbucks round the corner."

"I think I should wait for the police," he replied, swaying from one foot to the other uncomfortably. He was clearly not accustomed to being asked out for coffee. After a few seconds, he muttered, "Perhaps you'd like to come in?"

I followed the shy, middle-aged bachelor inside, remembering the chaos that was about to greet me. The thought of coffee made in Barclay's kitchen was repulsive, but how else could I keep the guy talking?

The house was even more disgusting by daylight, if that was possible. Barclay was a serial hoarder, and he was desperately searching for a space where I could sit down. He cleared a small area at one end of the sofa, relieving it of a stack of magazines, which he disposed of on the carpet beneath. I could hear him busying in the kitchen, and then he appeared with a small tray, on which sat two mugs of coffee and a plate of chocolate cookies.

I never actually drank the coffee, holding the mug to my lips and pretending to sip. I hardly knew the guy; he could have spiked my drink. Either that, or I could contract a bacterial disease from the unwashed china.

I wanted to engage Barclay in conversation about the child disappearances when he was a boy.

At first, he sat stiffly on a dining chair he had commandeered from the kitchen. He slurped his coffee and munched his way through the plate of biscuits, trying desperately not to make eye contact.

"You live alone?" I began.

"Since mother died, yes."

"Must be lonely. Got friends; got a girlfriend?" Barclay blushed at the prospect and shook his head.

"Look I hope you don't mind, but I was kinda bored waiting for you to get home, so I took a peek inside your diary."

Barclay became instantly defensive, stiffening in his seat, "You're not supposed to read someone else's diary; it's rude and disrespectful," he growled, his face turning a deep shade of purple.

"I'm sorry, but I was out there for hours waiting to do you a good deed."

Barclay calmed and drained his mug. He checked his watch, "What time did you call 911?"

"Oh, ages ago. They said they were busy and would get here as soon as possible." Of course, that sentence wasn't true, but Barclay didn't know that.

"Excuse my manners, I'm... Mary Goldstein," I proffered, producing the name of Noni's old canasta partner, the first name that popped into my head, "and you are?"

"Thomas. Barclay Thomas Junior."

In that moment, I realized that the man whose house I had invaded was not the correct Barclay Thomas but rather the son of our suspect. Nevertheless, his diary had been extremely useful.

"Well, very pleased to meet you, Barclay Thomas Junior."

"Likewise, Ms Goldstein," Barclay smiled reluctantly, apparently still uncertain as to why he had invited me into his home for coffee. It was probably the most adventurous thing he had done all year.

An awkward silence fell across the room, and then, "What do you do, Mary, as a job I mean?" Barclay had finally summoned the courage to ask a question.

"I'm a writer with the Sweet Water Tribune," I replied.

Barclay's ears pricked. Judging by the library of books and magazines strewn around his home, I had hit upon a certain passion.

"Really? How interesting."

I thought I had finally caught his attention, but the awkward silence returned.

"I'm currently working on a piece about the disappearance of several children from this area," I began.

Barclay was engaged at last; he sat bolt upright. My words had finally piqued his interest.

"You're a journalist?"

"You could say that, though I have yet to be officially given that title," I began, "I'm hoping this piece will be my paragon; that's why it's so very important that I report the details correctly."

Barclay seemed sympathetic to my plight, nodding his head in agreement. "It was a terrible time, I myself had a friend who went missing. He was never found."

"Oh, my goodness. How awful. I don't suppose you would tell me about your friend? It might be very helpful to my investigation," I pleaded, flashing my most endearing expression his way.

"Well, it was a long time ago; my memory has faded," he answered, rubbing the back of his neck nervously.

"Anything at all you can remember would be helpful," I encouraged, "let's start with your friend's name."

"Egan Reid," he reminisced, "my best friend. We bonded immediately. Egan made going to school more tolerable for me, and then one day, he disappeared, and I never saw him again."

Barclay cut a vulnerable figure, and it was easy to imagine that as a child, he would have been a prime target for bullies.

"Any idea what happened to him, how he went missing?"

"He was taken from his bed in the middle of the night. The police were at a loss to explain it. There was no break-in or signs of forced entry. My father was convinced that our neighbor was involved."

"Your neighbor? Whatever made him think that?"

"I really don't remember; it was so long ago, but I do remember the other kids at school called him the boogeyman."

"That name implies he was frightening. Was he?"

Barclay pondered for a moment, "He wasn't so much frightening as different. He was of Nigerian descent, but his skin was pale, his hair blond, and his eyes bright blue, an unusual combination for an African man. He always appeared awkward, as if ashamed of his appearance, and that made him the subject of idle gossip. I guess he stood out when really he wanted to blend in. I know exactly how that feels," he added pitifully.

"He was an albino," I declared.

"Yes, I suppose he was," acknowledged Barclay thoughtfully.

"Your neighbors were the Hempells, right?"

Barclay nodded.

"Didn't their son go missing too?" I prompted, remembering the third Hempell grave.

"That's right, he did."

"And your father thought Mr Hempell had abducted his own son?"

"Maybe. I'm not certain. My memory isn't as sharp as it was."

"Can you remember the child's name? That would be extremely helpful," I begged.

Barclay thought for a moment, then began routing through the piles of disorganization. In a flurry of old books that appeared to be photo albums, he tugged at one: his yearbook. He offered me the stained and tattered remnants of his childhood.

"Towards the back," he urged, "middle row, read the names."

From left to right, I read aloud the names of Barclay's peers, "Barclay Thomas, Egan Reid, Jenny Weaver, and Byron Hempell."

"That's it. Byron. Byron Hempell."

"Byron Hempell was in your year?" I questioned, as Barclay's diary entry had stated that he had never met Byron in person.

"He was supposed to be, but he was homeschooled. For some reason, his photograph popped up in our yearbook. None of us knew how."

"You must have been scared, I mean going to bed at night, knowing there was a predator in your neighborhood?"

"I was. Every kid was except for Frankie."

"Frankie?"

"Just a kid at school. He had a theory about everything, but no one took him serious."

"What was Frankie's theory about this?"

Barclay smiled as if the thought of Frankie rekindled fond memories, "Oh, he thought the predator was a vampire that only came out at night to take the children as a sacrifice and drink their blood." Barclay laughed at his words, "Silly, but kids and imagination equals wild, scary stories. All part of childhood, I guess."

"Was Baxter Hempell the vampire?"

"No. Frankie thought that Baxter took the children to give to his father to sacrifice."

This was beginning to get more interesting. Trying to maintain a calm, professional air, I asked, "Who was Baxter Hempell's father? Can you remember his name?"

"I never laid eyes on him. No one did, which only fueled Frankie's theory. His name was unusual, not American either; it had something to do with the moon, I think."

"If no one saw this man, how did you know he even existed?" I queried.

"Frankie said he saw him at the bedroom window standing behind Byron."

"Did you think Frankie was correct, or did you have your own explanation as to who was taking the children?"

The question was important, and I watched closely as Barclay grappled for the answer.

"As a kid, I believed Frankie, but honestly, in reality and in adulthood, I have no idea. It's not something that I've thought about for a very long time."

My chat with Barclay had been more helpful than I'd imagined. I thanked him for the coffee, which was still sitting, now cold, where he had placed it over an hour earlier.

"It's been a good chat, Barclay, but I must run."

Barclay saw me to the door. He looked almost disappointed that I was leaving. I turned back, and his face lit with anticipation before I said, "One last question. Where is your father?"

Barclay was overshadowed by disappointment once more as he answered somberly, "He died many years ago—why?"

"No reason, you just never mentioned him, that's all."

"Say, how do I contact you if I remember anything else?" he queried.

I wrote my cell number on the back of his hand and left.

Chapter Seventeen

Marie Richards was coming home from hospital. I rallied the kids to make her a 'welcome home' banner, but Tate was reluctant to hang it in their own home.

"Can't we just stay here?" pleaded Tate, realizing that his mother's homecoming meant going back to their own house.

"I want to go home," revealed Victoria sulkily, the privilege of a five-year-old.

Tate glanced from her to me and shrugged. He was too proud to beg, but his expression signaled exactly where he wanted to live.

"It's not up to me where you guys live; when your mom gets home, she's in charge." Roxy and Connie had agreed to place the banner in the Richards' home and get the place ready for Marie's return. I hadn't enlightened them as to my worries about that house. I thought it best to keep that to myself, erring on the side of, *What you don't know about doesn't worry you.*

It was a happy reunion between Marie and her children, and she seemed relieved to have left the hospital behind, though the drive home was one of mixed emotions.

As I pulled onto their driveway, the car fell into silence. No one rushed to get out. Everyone sat staring, the atmosphere fraught with tension.

Suddenly, Roxy appeared at the door, rushing towards the car in excitement.

"What are you waiting for, guys? Come on in."

A slow exodus of unease and apprehension sauntered towards the house. Painted smiles hid the underlying feelings of dread that I sensed within them.

Roxy ushered them inside, thrilled to show off the homemade banner and the result of her shopping trip to Walmart. She was completely unaware of the hesitancy in her guests.

Connie, on the other hand, was well aware of the disturbing atmosphere and the foul smell that had taken over the Richards' home.

She pulled me aside, "I don't like this house, Leni. I feel like something is watching me. It's like a dark cloud hovers over it, and it smells bad too."

I didn't unpack the car, because I had a feeling the backpacks and bags of laundry would be making another journey.

Marie looked pale, and though she managed to prize the semblance of a smile for her excited host, it was obvious she wanted to be anywhere but back in that house.

"Look, if it's too soon to be back here, there's room at my house," I offered.

It took less than a second for Marie to answer. She hugged me close. "Thank you," she whispered, "let's go."

Connie grabbed Roxy, the bottle of freshly opened prosecco, and a couple of plates of food and headed for the door.

"Where's Victoria?" questioned Tate.

Marie spun round, realizing her daughter was absent. A look of terror crossed her face as she directed her gaze towards the staircase. Victoria would probably be in her bedroom.

Tate stood firm, not offering to search for his little sister.

"Take your mom to the car; I'll go look for her," I instructed. The words were leaving my lips before I had a chance to stop them. The last thing I wanted to do was visit Victoria's bedroom again, but Connie and Roxy had already left, and Marie was too weak. I raced towards the second floor and turned towards the little girl's room. The door was closed, but a light shone from beneath it. I tapped quietly and whispered her name. There was no reply. I turned the handle slowly and pushed. Victoria was sitting on her princess coach bed, partially hidden by the parade of pink satin that decorated it. I could hear her talking. I approached stealthily, pulling aside one pink curtain and peering inside. Victoria was holding the shrunken head in both hands and chatting happily. She caught sight of me and jumped from the bed, tossing the head into the air before racing from the room.

I turned to follow, crying out as excruciating pain stabbed at my ankle. Blood was staining the top of my white sneaker, seeping from a wound just above the bone. I dabbed at the red discharge, eager to know what was causing such awful discomfort. The impression of a bite mark had torn into and broken the skin. What could have bitten me with such violence and force?

I searched the carpet for signs of the culprit, now remembering the shrunken head as it sailed through the air and dropped to the floor beside me when Victoria had slung it.

It certainly wasn't there now, but the faintest trace of blood spots marked a pathway towards the bed and disappeared. I peered beneath, spying the grotesque object lying out of reach. Its leathery, distorted features stared back at me, a drop of fresh blood drying in the crease of its shriveled mouth. I retched at the realization that I had been attacked by such an atrocity.

I rushed from the house and drove away, not caring whether I had secured the door behind me.

"What's happened? Why are you bleeding?" questioned Tate.

I glanced over my shoulder to where Victoria sat quiet and still beside her mom.

"Did Victoria do that?" he pleaded.

"No, no she didn't. It was that plaything of hers."

Tate glanced at his mom and back at me, "The head did that!" he gasped with amazement.

"Well, it was the only thing with blood around its mouth."

We swung into the driveway of Noni's, and I hobbled inside.

"Oh, my God, why you bleeding?" cried Connie, helping me onto a chair and elevating my leg on a mountain of cushions.

"It's nothing, just a scratch," I consoled.

"Roxy, fetch the first aid tin."

Connie bathed away the remnants of dried blood and applied antibiotic cream, wrapping the bite mark in a layer of crepe bandage.

"Perhaps you should get a tetanus shot," she advised.

"I'm sure I'll be fine, Con, but thanks for the concern."

That evening, Marie and Victoria retired to bed early. Victoria had said nothing and hardly eaten since the incident in her bedroom. Marie was weak and exhausted, bearing not only a physical wound but a heavy psychological one. It isn't every day a husband threatens his family with a gun and winds up in a hospital for the mentally ill.

Tate was happily washing dishes and chatting as we sat in our usual places around the kitchen table.

Sonia appeared with homemade cookies, and conversation turned to Barclay Thomas.

I recounted my conversation with the lonely bachelor and the details of Baxter Hempell's father, whose existence was either fact or fiction. I really wasn't certain.

Sonia agreed to investigate the elusive relative as well as check out the time of day the children disappeared.

Tate, who was listening intently, jumped into the conversation and asked, "Are you talking about the people who lived in the house before us?"

"Yeah, the Hempells," I replied.

"There's a ton of stuff in the attic that belongs to them. Mom never got round to throwing it out, but there could be something useful up there."

That was a great idea though,for some reason, no one seemed overly eager to check it out, especially at night! It was probably a job best left for daylight hours.

"What happened over there, Tate?" asked Connie gingerly, "I mean that night with your dad!"

"To be honest, I'm not even sure. When we moved in, everything was great, but a couple of weeks later, things started happening, and the feel of the place changed."

"Are you happy to talk about this?" I didn't want Tate to feel bombarded into answering questions that made him uneasy.

"Yeah, it actually helps to be able to talk about it, especially to people who aren't gonna think you're crazy."

"Crazy, crazy!" teased Roxy, "we're all crazy here."

"It started first with noises, knocking mostly, then footsteps, then voices. The knocks became bangs, really loud bangs, and they'd continue all night. No one was getting proper sleep. Dad stayed at work as much as he could; he hardly came home. Mom would buy flowers in the morning, and by the afternoon, they were dead. Fresh fruit decayed overnight. Then came the smell. It was worse upstairs, especially in Victoria's room. Mom and dad started arguing about everything. The house was turning everything rotten, including the people who lived there."

"You and Victoria—how did it affect you?"

"Victoria took to talking to an imaginary friend, her way of coping, I suppose. I felt like I was living in a parallel universe with people I didn't even recognize. I started having really vivid dreams, black ones, y'know, about killing people. I got scared to go to sleep."

Connie offered Tate a cookie.

"You said you heard voices—did you ever see anyone?" I questioned.

Tate thought for a while as he munched his way through a second cookie, "I heard Victoria talking to someone, but whenever I went into her room, there was no one there. Mom said it was imaginary, but I wasn't so sure. I did see a shadow moving behind her door, the light was always on, but there was never anyone else there, just Victoria curled up in bed."

"That's just too spooky for my liking," added Sonia, "no wonder you're not in a hurry to go back there."

"Where did Chase get the gun from?" queried Roxy.

"He had always had it, but he kept it locked in a security box. It was 'just in case,' he said, 'you never know when it might come in useful.'"

"When I spoke to him before the police arrived, he kept repeating, 'I didn't want to hurt her.' Who do you think he was talking about?" I asked.

Tate pondered the question, biting at his bottom lip nervously, "It sounds like he meant mom, but..."

"But what?" I demanded. I couldn't allow him to end his sentence with a 'but' and no explanation.

We waited for Tate to deliver. We did not anticipate it to be quite so shocking.

"I had noticed that dad had started to avoid Victoria. If she came into the room, he went out. When she spoke to him, he didn't answer. She stopped joining us for dinner. It was strange, like we were suddenly just a family of three. Mom drank in the evening; she never noticed the change in the father-daughter relationship.

"One night, I'd gotten up for a drink. It was late, early hours. I saw dad leading Victoria out of her room. He paused at the top of the staircase and lifted her into his arms. He seemed tormented, angry, and he was crying. I watched him position her over the balustrade, and I swear he was about to let her drop. I stopped him just in time. I'll never forget the look on his face, the anguish in his eyes, and the words he mumbled, 'I didn't want to hurt her.'"

A wave of audible gasps circled the table.

"So, you're saying it was Victoria your dad tried to hurt?"

"Yes, that's exactly what I'm saying."

Tate had finally given into his tiredness and wandered to bed. His startling revelation had impacted everyone, and it had taken quite a while for the topic of conversation to change.

I sat silently, deep in thought, as the others chatted around me.

"I think this family needs help, real help," I stated suddenly.

"What do you suggest?" asked Sonia.

"What kind of help?" queried Roxy.

"We will help them all we can," added Connie.

I smiled, "The help they need, we can't give them, Con. I've been thinking about it for a while, but after our conversation with Tate, I can't put it off any longer."

"Do you know of someone, Leni?"

"Yes, I think I do. We need…"

"The Pope," interrupted Roxy.

"The next best thing: Reggie Goodman."

Chapter Eighteen

Reggie was delighted to hear my voice; it had been way too long since we'd made contact.

We met Reggie at college, Roxy, Connie, and I. He became our fourth musketeer. He was funny, dependable, energetic, and Catholic, all the necessary virtues I decided were needed to help the Richards family.

I ferried Marie to the psychiatric unit in Frank's Town, where Chase was an in-patient. The local judge had ordered an assessment of his mental health before his release. His good standing in the community, and the fact that this was his first and only offense, meant Chase was likely to receive a verdict of community service for his misdemeanor, but only if he was deemed to be of sound mind. The unit itself was a modern, purpose-built structure that housed a total of thirty patients.

Chase was sitting in the open lounge area, playing backgammon with another man. He quickly abandoned the game when he realized that Marie was standing in the room. He hastened towards her, but Marie took a couple of steps backwards as he approached. Chase, unperturbed by her discouraging behavior, led us into a nearby conservatory where comfortable chairs had been positioned to view the immaculate expanse of garden beyond.

I felt somewhat awkward, a third wheel, though Marie had insisted that I accompany her rather than waiting in the parking lot.

"It's good to see you," began Chase, smiling pleasantly at his wife.

Marie did not respond.

"You're looking well, Chase. How's it going in here?" I felt compelled to engage in conversation in a bid to ease the tension.

"I think it's going good, thanks. I'm making progress, and I'm feeling much more like my old self."

"That's great, so nice to hear. Don't you think, Marie?"

Marie didn't answer. She rose from the chair and crossed slowly to the window, staring at the view.

"Beautiful, isn't it?" Chase said as he moved to her side. Marie stepped backward, turning to face him, and slapped his face with all the strength she could muster.

A man in a white uniform rushed towards them, but Chase stopped him with a wave of his hand, "It's okay, man, I deserved that." He then turned to Marie and asked, "Feel better now?"

Anger glowed in Marie's eyes; she'd been waiting a long time for that moment. The hurt that had festered inside her was now imprinted on Chase Richards' left cheek.

"Why would you do that to us? What were you thinking, Chase? You scared us all. I thought you were going to kill us. Whatever possessed you?"

Chase took a seat, "Honestly, I don't know, and that's the truth. I didn't feel like it was me. Sounds crazy, I know. I guess that's why I'm in here. I felt compelled to do it, like someone else was controlling me, telling me to hurt..." Chase cradled his face in his hands as the tears flowed.

"Telling you to hurt who?" demanded Marie. Chase was sobbing uncontrollably, but Marie stood firm, eyes glaring, waiting for the answer. "Well?" she growled.

Chase glanced towards her, then to me and back to her, his face contorted with anguish as tears clouded his vision, "Victoria..."

Marie faltered against the window, steadying herself against it. Tate was right. Victoria was Chase's intended victim. It had been hard enough for me to hear, and I could not begin to imagine how Marie felt.

There had to be an explanation. Chase Richards was not the sort of man to wake up one morning and decide to kill his daughter. He was a responsible, caring pillar of the community and a highly respected doctor. He wasn't a child killer; it didn't make any sense.

Marie had heard enough, and she left the room in a hurry. I placed a hand on Chase's shoulder and said, "Tell me, Chase, was it something to do with the house?"

Chase nodded. "I thought I heard a voice telling me to do it over and over again. I was so tired of listening to it, so confused. I just wanted it to stop. You have to believe me."

"I do believe you, Chase."

Marie was leaning against the car, her eyes red and swollen.

"Can you believe what he just said?" she asked. "How can I ever accept him back into our lives? How can I trust him again?"

"You will learn to trust him, but it's gonna take time. Look, I don't believe it was Chase holding the gun that night. There's something living in your house, something... evil. You feel it, the kids feel it, we all feel it. Why else would you be bunking with me when you have a beautiful home of your own? Admit it, you're afraid to go back."

Marie nodded.

"I should have known, should have seen it, Leni. What kind of mother am I? Instead of protecting my family, I pretend like everything's fine and grab the nearest gin bottle to disappear into."

"I don't think it's that simple, Marie. You're being very hard on yourself. You're not dealing with something normal here, this thing isn't rational, it's devious and malevolent. Its sole purpose is to inflict pain and suffering, and from where I'm standing, that's exactly what it's doing."

Marie looked frail and helpless.

"What do you suggest, Leni? How do I make this go away? How do I get my family back, get my life back?"

"Don't worry, Marie. I'm going to do everything I can to help you," I soothed.

"Yes, you can talk to it, can't you? You have that gift." Marie appeared excited, as though she had found the answer to her own question.

"I'm afraid not. It doesn't work like that. I'm a medium, a conduit between the dead and the afterlife, and that's where my purpose ends."

Marie was disappointed.

"Cheer up," I patted her shoulder gently, "I know someone who can help, and he's coming over later."

Chapter Nineteen

As the clock struck seven, Reggie was standing on the porch.

He was just as I remembered: tall and slender with a smile to light up Broadway. The tight curl of his Afro shaped and shaved to perfection. Reggie was a human firecracker, colorful, loud, and exciting. Positivity oozing from every pore.

Locked within his tight embrace, I breathed in his refreshing intoxication.

He bounced into the kitchen and into the arms of Connie, then Roxy.

I poured wine and dished up meatball spaghetti for supper.

Reggie entertained us with funny, animated stories about the life of a paranormal investigator for the Vatican. His raucous, high-pitched laugh bellowed throughout the house.

"God, I've missed you, Reggie," I announced.

"How could you not?" he roared, illuminating the room with the brightness of his smile.

"Now, Leni, the meatballs were delicious, Noni's recipe if I'm not mistaken, but you didn't bring me here just to sample your cooking, did you?"

The humor faded as the serious nature of Reggie's visit was about to be revealed.

"No, Reggie, I didn't. Truth is, I really need your help with something of a paranormal nature."

"Well, then shoot. I'm listening."

I poured forth the disconcerting events of the last few months, trying not to miss any detail.

Reggie's jovial demeanor changed; he became pensive, his expression solemn as the activities at the Richards' house unfurled.

"Sounds like you really do need my help," he remarked, tapping at his wine glass with a single finger.

"What do you think, Reggie? Can you help?" I was almost begging at this point, the desperation evident in my voice.

"Of course I can help, Leni, but what that entails, I'm not sure. I'm not a priest. I can't offer exorcism, but I can give you my honest opinion, and I do have contacts in the Church who I can call upon."

"Well, then that's a start," I sighed, refilling his glass.

At that point, I introduced the Richards. Their anxious, hopeful faces joined us around the table.

If there had been any doubt in Reggie's mind about his involvement, it was extinguished the moment he set eyes on Victoria.

"I'm gonna need to see the house," he began.

"Not a problem—that can be arranged. When are you thinking?" I quizzed.

"I'm thinking right now," he revealed. "No time like the present."

I scanned the row of startled faces, knowing the answer already, and asked, "Any volunteers?" After the inevitable silence, I added, "Looks like it's just you and me then, Reggie. I'll get my coat."

In the coolness of the evening, we crossed the yard and marched the acre of lawn that divided Noni's house from the Richards'. Reggie surveyed the building, which was cloaked in darkness except for the burst of light from a second-floor window.

"Anyone at home?" he queried.

"No. That's Victoria's room. Apparently, there's always a light on in there."

Minutes later, we were standing at the oak-paneled door as I fumbled for the key. My hand shook as the key clicked into place and unlocked the large door.

"Slightly nervous, Leni?" joked Reggie, taking my hand firmly in his.

A couple of steps, and we were inside. Reggie stopped abruptly.

"What's up?" I questioned.

"Did someone die here?"

"No, why?"

"That smell is hideous. I've come across such phenomena before but never so overpowering."

"It's always here, but it's stronger upstairs in Victoria's bedroom."

Reggie pinched his nose and flicked the light switch. Nothing happened.

"Electric off?"

"Don't think so, could just be a breaker."

"Not in my experience," he added.

At the foot of the stairs, he stopped again, "Do you feel that?"

I glanced towards him, "Like you're being watched?"

"Yeah, exactly like that."

"Always when I'm in this house," I replied.

It was difficult to focus through the darkness, every corner of the Richards' home playing tricks, deceiving the eyes, conjuring thoughts of unspeakable horrors lurking in the shadows.

Reggie spied the dead flowers and rotten fruit.

"This is worse than I thought, Leni. I think I need to contact the Vatican."

No sooner had Reggie spoken than his feet left the ground, and he flew into the air above me, legs dangling, arms outstretched, hanging like a human crucifix. The Bible in his pocket fell to the ground with a thud. I jumped backwards, scrambling for my cell, lighting the space around me with its meager glow.

"Reggie?" I cried from the shadows, turning the light upwards and searching for Reggie's face.

A strange gurgling sound was struggling from his mouth as he wrestled for breath. His eyes bulged, his mouth contorted, as if an unseen force was squeezing the life from his body.

I raced towards the open door, but it slammed shut in front of me.

My hand was trembling with fear as, in the glow of the torchlight, I caught sight of Reggie's body as it rotated in midair. Hovering upside down now, his head six feet off the ground.

I didn't know what to do. I spied the bible lying open on the marble floor and dashed to claim it, reading aloud from the passage that lay before me, my words flowing faster and louder as I wrestled to free Reggie from his nightmare.

Whatever held him hostage became angered by the chant of biblical words and hurled Reggie across the room, smashing him against the furthest wall. He crashed to the ground in a heap of tangled limbs.

I headed towards him as he lay unmoving, but a strong grip grabbed the collar of my coat, holding me stationary. Suddenly, I was racing backwards at great speed, being dragged with intimidating force up the staircase, screaming as I bumped against the rim of each step. I cried out to Reggie, who lay motionless where he had fallen.

At the top of the stairs, I was changing direction, my heels burning as I dragged track marks through the pile of the carpet. I crashed against a wall and hit the ground with a thud. Scrambling to my feet, I raced towards the open door. I was too late. Pulling at the handle, I prayed for the knob to turn, but the door had locked. I was trapped inside.

The room was Victoria's, the pungent odor overwhelming. I wrestled with the window; it didn't open,

I remembered. Grabbing the nearest object, I launched it at the glass. A small crack appeared on impact, but nothing more. As I searched frantically for a weapon, the door of the room flew open, and Reggie was standing there.

"Quickly, let's go," he beckoned, and we tumbled down the staircase together, missing steps in a desperate bid to escape.

A blast of night air hit my face. We were outside, collapsing onto the grass. The front door slammed so hard it punched through the quietness of the sleepy street like a boxer's knockout blow.

Only the rasp of our desperate, heavy breaths was audible in the silence. We staggered upright and hurried towards the safety of Noni's. I glanced back towards the house. Silhouetted in the window of Victoria's room stood the haunting figure of Jimmy Kale, but he was not alone.

In the security of the kitchen, we caught our breath. Reggie was nursing his left arm; his head was bloody, and a grape-colored swelling bulged from his right cheek.

My head hurt, and the heels of my feet were bleeding inside my sneakers.

"What the hell," remarked Reggie, the hint of a smile crossing his lips, "you're definitely gonna need extra help with this one, Leni."

"It's getting stronger, more malevolent; it's never physically hurt anyone before," I declared.

"Quick thinking with the bible; think you might just have saved my life," stated Reggie.

"You're welcome," I grinned. "Just like old times, never a dull moment with me around."

"You can say that again."

In the chaos of the Emergency Room, we sat like stunned rabbits waiting in turn for medical attention.

As Reggie returned from X-ray, I was replaying Victoria Richards' voice on the message Tate had forwarded.

He began to snigger, "Haven't heard that language in a long time."

"You recognize it?"

"Sure, I do. That's English Creole; my father tried to teach me, but I couldn't get the hang of it. Whose voice is that anyway?"

"That's Victoria Richards."

Reggie was stunned into silence.

With the ruptured ligaments of his left arm cradled in a sling, I drove Reggie home.

I knew the morning would unveil a map of bruises across the length of my back. An egg-sized lump had appeared on the back of my head, and my heels were sore.

I left Reggie just as the first rays of daylight claimed the morning.

"I'm so sorry I got you involved in this," I stated regretfully.

Reggie exited the car with a soft smile, "I'd like to say it was a pleasure," he joked. "Don't let the family go back to that house. It isn't safe."

"I won't, don't worry ... and thanks for tonight."

"I'll be in touch soon."

Chapter Twenty

Briefly, life assumed a semblance of normality.

The Richards kids returned to school, and Marie busied herself around the house, keeping Noni's pristine.

Sonia was busy at the library, and I needed to throw myself back into work. I'd had so much time away from my desk that colleagues were beginning to think I'd moved on. I was reminded of that traumatic night spent with Reggie every time I looked in the mirror. The tie-dye myriad of colors fading on my skin were a painful memento.

A week later, Reggie called.

"Hey, how's your arm doing?" I enquired.

"It's getting there thanks to the Vicadol. Man, you should see the color of it; ain't no color palette in existence that's not painted on my arm right now," he chuckled.

"Same here—my back looks like a Michelangelo masterpiece."

"We were lucky; could've been a lot worse. Still haunts me, that house," shared Reggie.

"Yeah, me too. Speaking of luck, I was hoping you'd had some with the church?"

"You read my mind, Leni. Oh, but wait, that's what you do, right?" Reggie taunted, "I've spoken with Father Yakub, explained the situation, and he's taken it to Cardinal Matteo. The Cardinal was apparently skeptical owing to the lack of physical evidence, but he's agreed to send two archbishops to investigate further."

Reggie paused momentarily, "Not exactly the answer you were looking for, I know, but hey, it's a start."

"Yeah, thanks, Reggie. Any idea when these two archbishops are planning to visit? Just want to be around when they do," I explained.

"I'm waiting for a call. Hopefully, I'll know later today. I'll text you.

That evening, as the last flicker of daylight disappeared, I bathed in the warmth of silky bubbles, soothing my bruised body and fading bite mark in honeysuckle bath salts. A choir of flickering candles sang in the darkness, and I savored every moment of tranquility.

As the water chilled and the glowing wax vanished beneath a dense blanket of steam, I stepped out, wrapping myself in a fluffy bathrobe. A flick of a switch, and the iridescent glow of electric light engulfed the room. I stood like always in front of the mirror, towel poised to wipe away its watery façade, when something stopped me. A finger message had been scrawled across its width and was rapidly evaporating before my eyes. The words read, 'DON'T WAKE THE MOON.'

Fear gripped my body as I rubbed frantically at the eerie words.

I called Sonia, hoping that perhaps the words meant something to her: the title of a book, a quote or phrase, but Sonia was as perplexed as I was.

The words played somersaults in my thoughts all night, and before I knew it, sunlight was dancing through the window. I spent the day at the office scribbling the words across a notepad, rearranging the letters in a desperate bid to make sense of them. What did they mean?

At lunchtime, Sonia called, "Hey, I've made headway in the search for Baxter Hempell's father," she exclaimed.

"Okay, great."

"It appears that Baxter Hempell was raised by his father, except he wasn't his father in the biological sense."

"Who was he then?" I queried.

"I'm not entirely certain of how he became Baxter's guardian. That will take more research, but I do have his name: Mahru Iwuagwu."

"African?"

"Yes, now here's the stinger: Mahru translates to 'face of the moon.'"

I pondered Sonia's words, the meaning of the African name, and the watery message. There had to be a connection.

I recalled my conversation with Barclay Thomas, "Mr Moon," I shrieked, and every head in the office turned to stare at me.

"Who's Mr Moon?"

I lowered my voice and said, "Barclay Thomas told me that Byron Hempell's grandfather was known to the locals as 'Mr Moon.' Perhaps we're getting somewhere, Sonia."

"Maybe, but I don't really see the relevance of 'Mr Moon'."

"Perhaps it isn't relevant at the moment, but I feel like there's some kinda connection. Keep digging, see if you can find any photographic evidence of Baxter's father."

"Okay! By the way, Eric was asking about you last night."

The mere mention of Eric's name whipped up a storm of emotions in the pit of my stomach. I tried to remain aloof, "All good, I hope?"

"Of course. He was asking about the investigation and whether we needed his help with anything else?"

I was slightly disappointed that Eric's interest was fueled by my ongoing search for the fate of nineteen missing children. However, I was happy to accept any modicum of interest that Eric might afford me.

"I really want to take a look in the Richards' attic. There could be something about Baxter's father up there. I can't think of anyone else willing to accompany me except for Eric. Do you think he would?"

"I'm sure he would," came the response, "but are you sure you want to go back there after what happened the other night. I mean, is it safe?"

Sonia's concern was affable, "No, I don't think it's particularly safe, but Eric owns a gun, right?"

Sonia hesitated. She was not one for unnecessary adventures, "I'll ask him," she sighed, "but personally, I think you should wait until after the archbishops have visited."

I reluctantly agreed. My haste to see Eric again could put both of us in danger.

Chapter Twenty-One

With Barclay Thomas no longer at the top of my suspect list, only one name remained: Erasmus Cobb.

Eric had discovered that Mr Cobb had served time for attempted child abductions and the possession of pornographic images of children. He was what the police termed 'a Chomo'—in layman's terms, a child molester, sexual predator.

Erasmus Cobb certainly possessed the credentials to be our perpetrator, though he never succeeded in his abductions and had no history of premeditated violence or actual sexual assault.

Erasmus, like Barclay, was a loner, passing through the childcare system like an unwanted gift. Devoid of family and friends, he wandered the streets of Manhattan, sleeping in doorways and on vacant park benches.

From his police headshot, it was difficult to determine his age. Overgrown, matted facial hair, years of self-neglect, and a brutal keloid scar down his left cheek completed his unsavory appearance.

After five years behind bars, he emerged hairless with the possibility of a trade in computing. He secured himself a job, rented an apartment, and became a mundane citizen.

By day, he was Erasmus Cobb, data inputter. But by night, he was a child groomer, dark web user, and porn enthusiast.

He went back to prison for his copious collection of images and his involvement with a known gang of pedophiles.

Erasmus went free just three months before the first child, Jenny Weaver, disappeared in December 1967, and according to Town Hall records he still lived in the area today. He was now seventy-six years old and residing at St. Bernadette's Home for the Elderly, here in Sweet Water Bay.

I secured an appointment at St. Bernadette's, posing as an interested relative in search of safe accommodation for my aging Noni.

"So very nice to meet you, Miss Goldstein," announced Barbara Chambers, the in-house coordinator.

"Likewise, Mrs Chambers," I replied.

"Please call me Barbara. We don't believe in labels at St. Bernadette's; we're all just brothers and sisters here, one big happy family," she declared with an uncomfortable grin.

I followed the width of her green, plaid skirt into a comfortable lounge area at one end of the building.

"Our relaxation room," she announced, sweeping the air with her hand like a ballerina.

"Very nice," I smiled, though there was nothing nice about it at all. The room was dimly lit and cluttered with threadbare armchairs. A solitary woman was asleep by the window that leeched the tiniest sliver of sunlight from a gap between heavy drapes.

"This way to the dining area." Barbara navigated a short corridor that opened into what resembled my school cafeteria. An army of white-coated individuals clattered and banged behind Formica worktops and glass-covered hotplates.

"What's on the menu today, Dorothy?" enquired Barbara.

"Same as yesterday: burger and chips," answered Dorothy with a nonchalant tone.

Barbara looked slightly embarrassed but proceeded to keep the dream alive by removing me as quickly as possible from the vicinity of the unenthusiastic Dorothy.

"Perhaps we can take a look at some bedrooms next."

Barbara directed me back into the corridor and down towards the opposite end of the building. Her pace quickened as we passed a couple of open rooms that were occupied. She stopped outside a closed door, announcing, "Here we are."

The room was beautiful, light, and airy, with flowery curtains and matching bed quilt. The furniture looked new and unused, and I suspected this was the room she showed all prospective relatives.

"Beautiful. I could see Noni in this room," I declared.

Barbara stuttered as she ushered me back towards the corridor, "I'm afraid this one is already taken."

"That's a shame, but you have more of the same?"

"Of course," she muttered with an underlying hint of insincerity.

"Now, unless you have any questions, I will see you out."

The whirlwind tour was over, and Barbara was desperate to see me out.

"How many residents live here?" I enquired.

"Twenty-two, though we have capacity for thirty," she informed, hastily directing me towards the exit. "If you're interested in a room, let me know as soon as possible. I'll forward the paperwork, and Noni will have a new home."

I wanted to reply, "Not in a million years," but instead, I smiled and thanked her for her time.

I heard Barbara sigh with relief as I turned to leave, but then I backtracked and caught her just before she disappeared into the nearest room.

She appeared disgruntled to find me standing behind her, displaying a disingenuous smile.

"One last thing, Barbara: I'd like to see a resident called Erasmus Cobb."

Barbara looked startled, stating, "In all the years Erasmus has lived here, you're the first visitor he's ever had."

As sad as those words sounded, it really wasn't a surprise, given the nature of his unsavory past.

"How do you know him? Are you related?" queried Barbara, whose interest was suddenly aroused at my request.

"Not exactly. He's an old friend of my grandpa. It would be lovely to see him after all these years."

Barbara eyed me suspiciously, and for a moment I thought she was going to decline, but then she ushered me down the corridor to room 32.

"He's in there. You have ten minutes," she announced, taking note of the time.

Behind the door of room 32 sat the possible murderer of nineteen children. I hesitated. Was I ready to meet him?

The smell hit me first, an overpowering mix of ammonia and excrement stinging at my eyes, intimidating my digestive system. My stomach wanted me to leave, but I fought the reflex, covering my mouth to ensure its contents didn't expel.

This room was nothing like the bright, flowery showpiece of earlier. Sparsely furnished, devoid of comfort, and resembling a prison cell rather than a bedroom. Maybe the man's past was known to his caretakers, and his surroundings were thought appropriate.

A small radio crackled on a bedside table, tuning was needed, and lying next to it, sparsely covered by bed sheets was the shape of an old man. I stepped closer until the wizened, weather-worn face of Erasmus Cobb was visible, his defining scar turned towards me.

"Mr Cobb," I whispered softly. He didn't respond.

I paused, hovering a hand above his arm, unsure whether to touch him or not.

"Mr Cobb," this time I gripped his bony forearm and shook him gently.

To be completely truthful, I was significantly relieved that the man in the bed did not awaken. My words would have been lost in the memory of his despicable actions, assuming, as I did, that he was the culprit.

I moved past the window, daylight fighting to enter the layers of grime and filth that shrouded it. A small sliver had broken through and touched the frame of a solitary photograph. Two men looked up at me: Erasmus, instantly recognizable with the facial lesion, and another man who would not have caught my interest if he had not been wearing a top hat.

I pushed the photograph into my purse and headed for the door, meeting Barbara on the other side.

I pushed past her and hastened to the exit as Barbara called out behind me.

Chapter Twenty-Two

The following day, Reggie advised that the archbishops were arriving from Rome that morning and would meet with himself and Father Yakub that evening.

"They will probably want to meet with you the day after," he stated. "Don't worry, I'll accompany them too," Reggie added, hearing the tension in my voice.

"I haven't gone to mass for such a long time," I admitted, "and confession, well, let's just say that the last time I went would have been around the time of Jesus himself."

Reggie was amused.

"Leni, stop stressing. They're not gonna worry about the last time you went to church. They are here to investigate the Richards' house and nothing more."

For the next couple of days, I stressed over the impending visit of such high-ranking members of the Catholic Church, whilst I waited impatiently for Reggie to get back in touch.

Eventually, the waiting was over as Reggie declared that Friday evening around 6pm would be good for the archbishops.

I raced home from work, showered, brewed fresh coffee, and had plates of sandwiches and cupcakes ready as they arrived.

"Should I curtsy on meeting them?" I questioned myself.

Before I could answer, they were at the door: two divine figures and Reggie.

"Please come in," I welcomed nervously, feeling like 'the big man himself' was entering my home.

"Let me introduce Archbishop Gregor Van Der Broek and Archbishop Luis Alvarez," began Reggie. "Bishops, my friend, Leni."

"Leni, that's an unusual name," announced Alvarez, "is it Spanish?"

"No, Father. It's Italian, short for Valencia."

"Ahh, I see. In that case, feel free to call us by our first names, Leni," he smiled.

Archbishop Alvarez was of Spanish origin, his dark hair and almond eyes, and the slightest hint of an accent, told me so.

Van Der Broek I assumed to be a Dutch name, though Gregor's accent was less definable. He was the exact opposite of his traveling companion, with blond hair and blue eyes.

Both men sat comfortably at the kitchen table and indulged in the delicacies I placed before them.

About an hour later, Father Yakub joined us, and though most of the food had been eaten by then, he indulged in the remaining cupcake and coffee.

"Isaac, my friend, thank you for joining us this evening," began Gregor. "Reggie tells me that this young lady needs the church's help. Are you up for a little exorcism?"

Isaac Yakub was a middle-aged man with a chiseled jaw line and emerald eyes. He resembled a game show host rather than a man of the cloth, and in my opinion was a sad loss to the female race.

"Absolutely, whatever you need, my child," he declared, holding my gaze in his. "But I thought that was the reason you had traveled here. It's been a long time since my last exorcism. I'm a little rusty."

"And even longer since ours," added Luis.

"The monsignor asked us to certify that such a decision was necessary. He spoke very highly of you, Father, and your past successes with such phenomena," boasted Gregor.

Father Yakub nodded graciously, accepting the compliment that had been bestowed upon him.

"Anything for the monsignor; it would be my honor," he replied.

"Excellent. We shall await the outcome before our return to Rome the day after tomorrow," informed Luis.

Formal niceties bounced awkwardly around the kitchen table from one priest to the other. I got the distinct feeling that the archbishops had jumped at the chance to take a trip abroad, knowing from the start that Father Yakub would be the chosen advocate to perform the ritual.

Father Yakub had been set up by his fellow clergy, though he found himself unable to turn the opportunity down, especially at the mention of the monsignor.

As the archbishops disappeared into the night, traveling by limousine to their luxury hotel, Father Yakub remained behind.

"Well, that went well," scoffed Reggie. "They stitched you up good and proper, Father."

Father Yakub's solemn expression turned to one of jovial laughter at Reggie's statement.

"Whisky or wine, Father?" I enquired, feeling that the moment called for one or the other.

"You do realize, Reggie, that every exorcist requires a second to accompany him, and you will be mine," declared the Priest.

Reggie's expression jumped from happy to anxious in a split second; his mouth gaped, and his eyes widened.

"Gotcha," hissed Father Yakub, swigging back the whisky and signaling for more.

We hit the whisky hard that night, drinking into the early hours. Father Yakub and Reggie resembled a double act. I had no idea that a Catholic priest could be so entertaining.

As the shadows of darkness lifted, Reggie and the priest said goodbye with the promise of returning the following week to evict the evil residing in the Richards' house.

The next morning, Eric arrived quite unexpectedly.

I was suffering the aftereffects of consuming a bottle of hard liquor the night before and answered the door in my robe, expecting to find the mailman. The sight of Eric threw my head into a spin; I played with my hair and rubbed the remnants of sleep from my eyes, trying to look as fresh as a hungover person can look.

"Eric, what brings you here so bright and early on a weekend?" I queried.

"Sonia said you needed my help."

I stared at him blankly, vaguely recalling said conversation.

"Oh, yes, of course. The visit to the Richards' house. Come in, let me make you breakfast."

I left him with coffee and pancakes while I showered quickly and applied a light makeup.

I had promised Sonia that no one would enter that house until after the exorcism, but Eric was here now, and it would have been rude of me to turn his offer down.

I tried to convince myself that the visit would be quick, but I knew in my heart that it would be quite the opposite.

"I think I should let you know about my last experience in the Richards' home," I began. "It didn't end well."

Eric listened to my story, his eyes growing wider with every word.

"Look, Leni. I don't believe in ghosts or the boogeyman. Whatever happened that night will have a perfectly reasonable explanation. I deal with facts. I promise you; nothing is going to happen."

I smiled meekly. Eric was in denial; he had no idea of what he was stepping into, and perhaps for him, that wasn't such a bad thing. For me, on the other hand, it could all end tragically.

Around mid-morning, as the Richards family headed for a day out at the local zoo, Eric and I walked the short journey to their house.

I had to admit that a morning spent nestled in the warmth of my duvet seemed a far nicer option, and I could feel my anxiety levels rising with every step closer to the malign dwelling.

Even in daylight, the house was oppressive. It loomed in front of us like a giant trap waiting to snare its prey. I knew we were being watched, but I kept that to myself.

Eric opened the door and stepped inside. I followed close behind.

The house was shrouded by darkness, its huge windows avoided by the warmth of the morning sun, as if the planet itself knew not to venture inside.

The air hung heavy, its overpowering stench more putrid and potent than before.

Eric gagged, "What the hell is that smell?"

I wanted to say, 'It's the smell of evil, of malevolence,' but instead I shrugged and said, "It was here the other night too; perhaps something strayed in and died."

"Sure smells like it," replied Eric, placing a hand to his nose.

We crossed the hall towards the staircase and looked upwards. "Ready?" I asked. Eric nodded and took my hand as we ascended to the next floor. Here, the smell was even stronger. Eric heaved uncontrollably, his face red from retching, his eyes watering from the sting of the odor.

"That isn't the smell of a dead stray," Eric protested. "I've smelled rotten flesh before."

We hurried across the landing and up the next set of stairs, the ones that led directly to the attic.

The house was awake now, aware of our intrusion. I could feel it stirring around us, pulsing to life. I wanted to head for the door, but Eric's strong grip was pulling me upwards, and before I realized it, we were standing at the attic door.

Here, the putrid smell was less potent, but the room throbbed to the beat of malevolence. Cloaked in darkness with evil intent lurking in every corner. I clung to Eric, every hair on my body chilled to attention, every breath shallow and labored.

Eric seemed unaware of my unease as he fumbled to retrieve a flashlight from his pocket.

"Bloody dark up here," he protested before proceeding to illuminate the recesses of the enormous space.

The attic was a treasure trove of antiquities and ancient relics.

"I feel like we've just discovered an archeological site," he mused, flashing light from floor to ceiling.

"We've discovered something..." I wanted to say, "...but exactly what remains to be seen."

I recognized the shields and spears from the Hempells' old living room and the chair that Cora Hempell had occupied beside the fire, now with only one shrunken head dangling at its side. In the deepest corner of the room sat a pyramid of deteriorating boxes; I tore at the top one, and it was filled with old books and manuscripts.

Pulling that box aside, I opened the next, which was filled with the jars from the Hempells' sideboard, thick black liquid hiding all manner of inexplicable contents.

"What the hell are they, Leni?"

"No idea, Eric, and if I'm being honest, we probably don't want to know."

"Should I call in forensics, get them tested?"

"Maybe—let's just see what else we find."

I was as eager as Eric to know what lurked in the depths of the unmarked jars, but I also knew that removing them from the house would not be prudent.

The forces around us were agitated; I could feel their distaste. They lurked in the shadows, fighting to escape, but they were trapped, imprisoned by the same force that held Jimmy Kale.

I was beginning to feel anxious now, the room was getting hotter, and sweat was forming on my brow. An incessant buzzing was growing above our heads. Eric shone his torch upwards toward the angled ceiling, where a swarm of flies circled a single bulb hanging there, as if drawn to the light. Except there was no light.

Suddenly, in one swift change of direction, they dived towards us, clinging to our hair, crawling across our skin, relentless in their frenzied attack.

Eric grabbed my arm whilst defending himself with the other and pulled me towards the attic door.

It slammed shut behind us. We were flailing in desperation, edging closer to the top of the staircase. The flies continued to attack, and then, in an instant, they were gone.

Jimmy Kale had stepped out of the shadows, his arms outstretched, welcoming the swarm to cover him.

A moment later. he disappeared, and the house was silent. Eric had witnessed firsthand the supernatural. His face was a pale shade of disbelief. He trembled visibly as he reached his hand towards mine.

We needed to leave. The house had spoken; we weren't welcome. Jimmy Kale had helped us, but I suspected that was where it ended.

"We need to go, Eric, now!" I growled.

He needed no convincing as we raced down the staircase together towards the front door, but the door wouldn't open. Eric banged and tugged at it feverishly—it was stuck firm. He grabbed his cell in desperation: no signal.

"Back way," he prompted, but the back door was stuck too.

Then he noticed another door leading from the laundry room.

"In here," he beckoned.

I followed closely as we disappeared down a narrow set of stairs opening into a wider space beneath. It seemed that we had hit a dead end, then suddenly, Eric disappeared. I crouched down to see the white souls of his sneakers crawling into the distance.

Enclosed spaces and I did not usually do well together, but there was no other option, and Eric, operating on adrenaline, hadn't seen the need to discuss the confined route before entering.

The tunnel was small, and the ground beneath my hands cold and damp. I screamed as a furry object scurried across my fingers. I soldiered forward, following the heel of Eric's shoe and the pinnacle of torchlight that wavered in the distance. The tunnel seemed infinite. I felt the surge of panic swelling inside as sweat caressed the back of my neck.

"Eric... Eric!" I shouted, suddenly realizing that Eric's shoe was no longer in front of me. I hurried forward, splinters stabbing at my knees, panic ready to erupt.

A moment later, the strength of Eric's arms were around me, pulling me towards him. I stumbled into him, the sweet aroma of his cologne a welcome, momentary distraction.

"Where are we?"

The room was large, perhaps half the size of the attic, but the fact I could stand up was a bonus.

"I'm not sure—it seems like an add-on, and there's a staircase over here. Perhaps we can get out this way."

I hesitated, but Eric and the torchlight were making their descent.

"What are you waiting for?" cried Eric, desperation in his voice. I followed blindly.

"Shine your light around the room; I want to see what this is," I instructed.

Reluctantly, Eric did as I asked. Torchlight scoured the walls, the ceiling, and the floor. The room was pretty bare except for a stone table in the center, a carved wooden sideboard, and a large metal bucket.

The table was heavily stained with dark, dried patches of red, particularly around the center where a round hole was positioned. Beneath the hole sat the bucket saturated with the remnants of what appeared to be dried blood. As Eric lowered the torch, a flash of white caught my eye. A huge, painted circle encompassed the table, richly decorated with symbols and dotted with melted candles.

"What on earth do you think this is?" I asked Eric, exploring the stone surface.

"If I had to guess, I'd say a mortuary table," he replied.

"Really? What makes you think that?"

"It resembles those at the mortuary, a much cruder model I admit, but the hole in the center is for drainage, and the bucket is to catch the blood."

Eric may be right, but what was it doing in there, and how did it get there?

I turned my attention to the sideboard, ancient-looking dark wood, draped in velvet, moth-eaten cloth. It was home to a collection of feathers and small bones and a long, rectangular box. Torchlight found its opening, and I turned the rusting key and peered inside. Lying in the shadow of its carved tomb was a shiny dagger with a smooth black handle.

Eric was at my shoulder, "What on earth…"

He bathed the knife with light; it lay cushioned on a crudely constructed rag doll. The doll had no eyes, and the mouth was a series of black cross stitches. I recognized its significance as those that plagued Jimmy Kale.

As disturbing as that discovery was, it wasn't the last. I removed the doll from its resting place and turned it over. Pinned to the back of its head was a photograph of Victoria Richards.

"Isn't that…?" queried Eric.

"Victoria."

In that moment, there was a loud bang and another. A sequence of them followed, each one louder than the one before. The candles on the floor flickered to life.

We raced up the staircase and didn't look back. Beneath the Richards' house, the maze of rooms and staircases made finding the exit confusing, but eventually we stumbled upon the basement. Eric searched for an exit; a flicker of daylight beckoned from a solitary window hidden beneath the chaos. The gap was small, but I eased through it with a little extra push from behind and fell into the open air, gorging on its freshness and running my fingers through the cool, moist grass beneath my body. I waited for Eric, but he didn't emerge. His face finally appeared, a look of despondency. He couldn't fit through.

"Come on, Eric, try. I'll kick in the frame if I have to."

"It's no use, Leni. I'll find a different way," and suddenly, he was gone.

I waited on the steps of the Richards' house, desperate for him to appear. I could've gone back inside, but the prospect was nauseating, even though it would be to save Eric. Just as I was about to give up hope, the front door opened, and Eric sauntered calmly through it.

"You took your time," I sighed, relieved to know that Eric was safe.

He smiled as if nothing had happened, "Don't know about you, Leni, but I could use a stiff drink."

Chapter Twenty-Three

Father Yakub had finally found time in his busy schedule to visit the Richards' house and penciled a date for the following Friday afternoon.

"I'm very grateful, Father, that the exorcism can happen so quickly."

"Perhaps exorcism is too strong a word to begin with, Leni. I will perform a cleansing. Usually that's all that is needed to evict unwanted spirits, and then if that doesn't work, we can look at exorcism," he explained.

I was slightly confused by the priest's words, having been reassured by the archbishops that an exorcism would be performed, but Reggie trusted in him, and I would too.

"Just one other thing. I am forbidden from entering the home alone—Vatican protocol. I will need to be accompanied; perhaps you would be so kind as to muster a volunteer."

I assured Father Yakub that he would not enter the house alone, already knowing that I would be his volunteer.

As much as we all loved the Richards family and had grown steadily attached to their existence, the house was beginning to feel crowded. Connie and Roxy felt unable to bring home casual acquaintances for fear of upsetting Marie or disturbing Victoria.

Tate left dirty socks, abandoned sneakers, half-eaten sandwiches and school textbooks in every room of the house.

To make matters worse, two days later, Chase Richards was discharged from the psychiatric hospital, which added one more person to the overcrowding.

Marie was totally against Chase living in such close proximity, but quite honestly, he had no place else to go. The kids were overjoyed that their father was coming home, neither aware that the night he wielded a gun, the bullet was intended for Victoria.

Chase was perched on the edge of his bed. He had no idea of what had been happening in his home and was under the assumption that he was returning there.

However, he settled into Noni's, taking refuge in the bedroom furthest away from Marie's. That room was Connie's, which meant she was bunking with me, again!

That night we dined together, seven of us around the kitchen table, sharing meatballs and pasta. Even Marie's frosty exterior melted away after several glasses of Italian wine.

As Chase left the table, he thanked me for my hospitality and the kindness I had shown to his family. He took himself off to bed with a gracious "Goodbye."

I awoke to the screams of a child echoing through the quiet of early morning. Victoria. Connie and I raced across the landing to the open doorway of Chase's room. Marie was on her knees at the side of his bed, cradling her sobbing daughter, as Tate looked on in disbelief.

Chase Richards was dead. The blue tinge of his lips and the stiffness of his posture being the symptoms of my diagnosis.

An empty bottle of pills lay beside him, washed down with his favorite whisky.

He'd left a note held in Marie's trembling fingers, a discarded envelope lying on the rug beside her.

"Marie, please do not hate me for my action. It is safer for you all if I am no longer around. I cannot promise that Victoria will remain safe, and I can no longer trust in my ability to do the right thing. I cannot explain the person I have become; I only know that I love you all. Maybe one day you will understand and know how sorry I am to leave you like this.

Always in my heart, Chase/Daddy xxx"

The scene was one of unimaginable sorrow. The Richards were devastated.

Chase was recovered by the coroner's office, and Eric and his colleague Mike took statements.

The whole sad affair was shocking and unexpected.

"It appears to be a straightforward suicide," stated Eric. "We'll perform an autopsy and let you know when the body is released."

It was a gray, gloomy day with heavy rain forecast as Father Yakub's black Mercedes swung onto the Richards' driveway.

My heart was pounding with a mix of trepidation and hope.

It was comforting to see Reggie emerge from the back seat of the car and follow the priest towards me.

For a moment, I prayed that he was the accompaniment Father Yakub had spoken about, but Reggie shook his head vehemently, "Ain't no way I'm going back inside that house, not even for you, Leni."

I nodded, glancing at the arm support Reggie still sported. His souvenir from our last visit.

"Thought you could use some moral support, though," he proffered.

"You know it," I replied.

Father Yakub, unperturbed by this latest venture, held a bible in one hand and a rosary in the other.

"My sword and my shield," he joked, "everything I need to go into battle."

"Come, Leni. Let's get this over with," he urged, stepping closer to the house.

I unlocked the door. The priest faltered, opened his bible, and stepped forward.

The house was unusually quiet as I stood beside the clergyman, bubbles of nervous tension forming across my brow.

I waited for chaos to unleash itself, but the house remained still, almost normal.

Father Yakub began chanting from his bible and signing the cross in midair. He walked from one room to the next, repeating his ritual. I drifted beside him, waiting for the shadows to move, the foul odor to strengthen, or a sign that confirmed the truth behind the priest's urgent visit, but there were none.

As we reached the attic I hesitated, remembering my last encounter. But the father entered without a second thought and paced its length, unhindered by the malevolence that nested there. "What happened?" queried Reggie as we emerged unharmed. Father Yakub closed his holy book and tucked away his crucifix.

"Nothing happened, Reggie, the house is cleansed," smiled the priest. "I don't think the family will have any more trouble."

It had been easy. Too easy. My relief was overshadowed by doubt.

Reggie shrugged, hugged me tightly, and followed Father Yakub to his car. The priest shook my hand politely and drove away.

I headed home with good news for the Richards.

A huge lightning storm hit Sweet Water Bay that night, and as bad as it was, it was only the beginning of a greater storm yet to come.

When Chase Richards had been laid to rest, the family packed up their belongings and headed home. It was an emotional goodbye for all concerned.

"Hey, guys, look—I'm only next door, you can still come visit." I comforted as Tate and Victoria clung to my body like leeches.

Marie was doing okay with the help of sleeping pills and Xanax. It pained me to see them go, but it was time for them to get on with their lives and I with mine. Perhaps now I could get back to investigating the missing children, something that I'd put on hold to deal with the Richards' plight and their uninvited guest.

Chapter Twenty-Four

"I can't believe it was that easy to rid the house of whatever was living there," stated Roxy.

"Me either," Connie added, "but boy am I glad it's over, right, Leni?"

I nodded compliantly, hiding the anxiety that was gnawing in the pit of my stomach. Why was it so easy for the priest to cleanse the Richards' house? I couldn't help my skepticism; I had a hunch that whatever it was would be back or actually hadn't left at all.

Connie mixed cocktails in celebration of our new-found freedom, and we sipped the night away under the influence of homemade mojitos and margaritas.

Around midnight, we staggered to bed; I collapsed into the comfort of waiting pillows and disappeared into sleep.

"It cannot be morning already," I moaned as the taste of stale alcohol repeated forcefully.

I cursed the brightness of the morning sun for disturbing me so early. I forced a squint at the clock: it was only 4 am, not morning at all.

The light dimmed slightly as I emerged from an avalanche of pillows to find Noni immersed in the brightness and sitting at the foot of my bed. My heart burst with happiness to see her smiling face and soft brown eyes once more. I sprang from the bed to embrace her, but she turned away as I approached.

"Noni," the word was desperate as it left my lips, "what's wrong?"

Noni stood slowly, her head drooped forwards, and in one swift movement, she launched herself towards me. It was no longer Noni as the disfigured face of Cora Hempell, arms outstretched, lunged into view.

I closed my eyes and screamed.

Connie was quickly at my side, always the lightest sleeper, "Leni, wake up! You're having a nightmare."

I opened my eyes as if it was the first time that night. The room was dark again, and the spirit had gone. The clock read 5:30 am. Perhaps it had been a nightmare and the visit from Cora Hempell never happened?

The following morning, I called at the Richards' house to find Marie in good spirits.

"Just checking on you guys," I proclaimed with a hint of trepidation.

"Everything's fine, thanks. Tate has walked Victoria to school, so I'm planning on a little housework," Marie advised. "Thank you again for everything, I, we really do appreciate it."

"Not a problem. You'd have done the same for me, right?" Marie nodded and smiled.

"It's high time I tackle that attic. I've been putting it off for far too long."

"Are you sure you're ready for that?" I questioned, drowning in a wave of nausea at the mention of the room.

The attic filled with the Hempells' creepy artifacts was certainly not the best place for Marie to visit alone.

"Stop worrying, Leni. I'll be fine. The house is clean now, remember?"

I set off to work with Marie's words reverberating in my thoughts. Did I believe her when she said she would be fine? Probably not. That niggling feeling was back. Noni always said, "Trust your gut instinct—it's always right." My gut instinct was turning somersaults.

I'd just reached the office when my cell phone rang.

"Is that Mary?" asked a quiet voice at the other end of the line. I was just about to say no, when I recognized the voice belonging to Bradley Thomas.

"Yes, this is Mary," I replied.

"Oh, good. It's Bradley Thomas; we met the other evening when my house had been broken into. Do you remember me?"

I hesitated for a couple of seconds, acting uncertain, "Er... yes, yes. I do remember you now. What can I do for you, Mr Thomas?"

"Well, you said to call if I remembered anything about the children who went missing years ago." My ears pricked up as I waited for him to continue. "I've remembered the name of Baxter Hempell's father."

My heart sank. Sonia had already established that information, but I didn't want to sound ungrateful. "Oh really, that's wonderful; well done," I encouraged. Bradley sounded delighted at the acknowledgment of his discovery. "Okay, so what is it?"

"I better spell it for you as I'm not sure how you would pronounce it. Have you got a pen?"

He spelled out the name for me, taking care over each letter.

"That's great, Bradley—I've got that now. Thank you for your call..." but before I could politely end the conversation, Bradley interrupted, "...that's not all; I was going through some old papers last night..." The vision of Bradley Thomas's living room with its library of books and papers popped into my head, "...and I found some old newspaper clippings about the disappearances. I thought they might be of value to you?"

"Absolutely. I could call round on my way home from work if that suits you?"

The phone went silent for a moment as Bradley pondered my proposal.

"I suppose that would be okay... though I had rather hoped to meet you somewhere—the diner in Walrus Bay, perhaps?" His voice waned with each word of the sentence as if saying it aloud was embarrassing.

Walrus Bay seemed a long way from home just to meet for some old scraps of newspaper.

"Maybe the diner in Sweet Water—the one by the coast, Sandpiper's, would be easier?"

Bradley accepted with a slightly disappointed tone.

"Shall we say 5:30 tonight, then?"

As I swung into the parking lot of the Sandpiper's diner, the image of Bradley Thomas was sitting hunched beside the window.

He recognized me instantly, his eyes growing wider, and a smile crossing his lips. I probably would have walked past him in the street, but the shabby beige overcoat and disheveled hair told me I was sitting opposite the right man.

"Lovely to see you again, Mary," he began.

I detected Bradley considered our get-together as something more than just a meeting to pass on information. Instinct told me he perceived it as a date.

The server instantly provided coffee and issued a menu.

"Anything you like—I'm paying," announced Bradley proudly.

"I'll take a club with fries please."

Bradley twitched nervously, wringing his hands constantly, his eyes only daring to meet mine for a fleeting moment.

"Relax, Bradley, this isn't a job interview," I joked, breaking the silence.

Bradley sniffed, a wry smile breaking the regimented line of his lopsided mustache.

He reached into the pocket of his heavily stained overcoat and pulled out a neatly folded handful of clippings. He placed them on the table as the server returned with more coffee.

She caught a glimpse of the dated newspaper and its headline.

"I remember that. Those kids going missing. My sister was one of them," she announced with a strangely casual tone.

"Oh, really? How sad, I'm so sorry. Was your sister found?" I queried.

"No. Never knew what happened to her. Broke my mother's heart it did. Long time ago now though."

"Do you mind if I ask your sister's name? I'm a journalist, and I'm investigating the case."

"Amanda Starling. Mandy, we called her." Her eyes glazed over as though she were reminiscing. "Have you any idea what might have happened to her?"

"Not really—she was taken from her bed during the night. No one could tell us how, no break in or nothing. Mom put her to bed as usual, and the next morning she was gone."

"Just like my friend Egan," added Barclay. "He disappeared from his bed."

"Yeah, they all did, hun. Every one of them," confirmed the server.

The look of ignorance on my face must have been obvious.

"Read the clippings. They all disappeared from their beds."

My shock was evident as I stared from the server to Bradley Thomas and back again.

I don't think we had reached that stage of the investigation; it was something that needed attention.

We knew the names of the children and where they lived; we knew their ages, the dates they disappeared, but we had omitted to determine their whereabouts at the time of their disappearances.

"You okay?" enquired the server. "You've gone a bit peaky."

I gulped at the refilled coffee and pored through the newspaper clippings one by one. There were ten paragraphs in all, neatly cut from the Sweet Water Tribune.

"Who cut these out?" I asked.

Bradley scratched his head and tugged at his mustache, "I guess one of my parents. They were in the back of an old scrapbook; it was a hobby of my mother's. Everyone took an avid interest in the children. It was shocking to the whole community." he reasoned defensively.

"And these are all you could find, just the ten?"

Bradley nodded.

"Mind if I keep them? They could be useful."

Bradley nodded again.

I finished eating and grabbed my bag.

Bradley looked somewhat disheartened as I pulled on my jacket and rose to my feet. I needed to get home and contact Sonia with my newfound information.

"Say, you ever heard of a guy called Erasmus Cobb?" I asked before departing.

"Got a photo?" queried Barclay. "The name's kinda familiar, but I'm much better with faces."

I did have a photo, the one I had stolen from the old man's room, but it was lying on the dresser of Noni's bedroom.

I shook my head as the thought of another date with Barclay forbade the truth.

"Thanks for the date. It's been fun," I winked playfully, throwing my purse over my shoulder. I headed for the car, leaving Bradley grinning like a Cheshire cat.

As I drove away, he was waving and still smiling.

Chapter Twenty-Five

Sonia was delighted and disappointed all at the same time by the additional information Bradley Thomas had provided.

"I can't believe we never thought to find out where the children disappeared," she moaned, "some detectives we are. It took a server in a diner to make us realize..."

"And now that she has, we can get on and find out, can't we?" I interrupted.

"Okay, Leni, you take the first ten, and I'll take the rest. I can feel a long night coming on."

I said goodbye to Sonia and headed upstairs. Some of my best thinking happened in bed. Armed with a laptop, a peanut and jelly sandwich and a double helping of Connie's best whisky, I set about my task. I was awoken rather crudely, not by the buzz of my monotonous alarm clock, but by the rocking and jilting motion of my body. Connie was the culprit, shaking me into consciousness with amazing force.

"What the hell, Con?" I scrambled to a sitting position.

"Quick, Leni, it's happened again," her tone was desperate.

I knew in an instant by the look on her face Connie had encountered the man in the top hat.

"He's in Victoria's room."

It was 4 am. Victoria would have still been sleeping. I hauled myself from the warmth of the duvet and padded across the landing to Connie's room.

Peering from her window directly across from Victoria's, I watched and waited.

"There's no one there, Connie,"

"He was, though, Leni. Honest. I woke for some water, and when I came back, I was looking out the window, and there he was, just standing looking back at me."

"Well, he's gone now…" just as the words left my mouth, the shadow of the man in the top hat crossed in front of Victoria's window.

"Oh, my God. You're right."

I raced down the stairs and out into the night, vaulting across the lawns and driveways to the Richards' house.

I banged at the front door feverishly.

Eventually, I heard a faint voice calling from above. Tate was hanging from his window, "What's up, Leni?"

"Tate, there's someone in Victoria's room. Let me in."

"What did you say?" queried the blurry-eyed teen.

"Never mind, just come down and let me in. It's urgent."

At that point, Marie opened the door, clutching a silk kimono to her chest, and asked, "What's going on?"

I rushed past her, almost knocking her over in my haste, and headed up the staircase to Victoria's room.

I fell through the doorway and almost onto Victoria's sleeping body, stumbling to regain my balance.

The little girl lay peaceful and quiet, unaware of my desperate intrusion.

Catching my breath, I glanced around the room. It was empty, no sign of the man in the top hat. I crossed to the window, where Connie had taken up residence. I waved calmly, indicating that my sudden, unexpected visit to the Richards' home in the middle of the night had yielded no intruder.

Connie waved back.

I was just about to turn away when a shadow passed behind Connie and paused. Panic stabbed at my gut, my heartbeat increasing rapidly as I realized that the shadow in my friend's bedroom was the man in the top hat.

I pointed frantically, stabbing the glass repeatedly, but Connie was unaware of the obtrusive figure. The man in the top hat lifted his cane and struck her violently across the back of the head, and she dropped from view instantly. He pressed his face to the window, fiery eyes glowing as he vanished into the night.

I sprinted home, leaving Tate and Marie in a state of shock.

"What's happening?" echoed their collective voices behind me.

At the top of the stairs, the door to Connie's room was open. Her legs were visible protruding from the end of the bed. I rushed to her side, where a halo of blood stained the rug beneath her. She was unresponsive, both eyes wide open, pupils fixed. I screamed for Roxy, who appeared seconds later.

"Call 911."

Roxy fumbled with her cell phone, trembling with shock.

"What's happened? Is she okay?"

Her questions were dulled by the numb sensation that coursed through my body. I couldn't answer; I couldn't speak.

Roxy knelt beside me as we waited for help to arrive. Neither of us daring to ask the question, too afraid of the answer.

Time stood still.

Finally, the paramedics arrived.

"She's breathing, but her pulse is weak," I heard one of them say.

Before we knew it, she was gone, flashing lights and sirens as her escort. Roxy and I hugged tightly as Connie's ambulance vanished out of sight.

"Follow on," they'd said, "Crowther's Bay General."

Those last few hours before dawn were nothing but a blur, a tornado of emotions as we waited for news of our friend.

Blue scrubs and white coats hurried back and forth along the corridor, and we looked on with desperation and hope that one of them was heading towards us, but the morning came and still we waited.

Marie arrived with coffee and pastries. We couldn't eat, or sleep, or find the energy to talk. We needed to know what was happening.

It didn't look good. Six hours earlier, she'd been taken into the operating room; it was now mid-morning, and we had heard nothing.

Then it happened: a tall, red-haired young woman with tired eyes and pale skin approached.

"Connie Hart, are you relatives?"

Stunned into the realization that she had mentioned Connie's name, I stuttered a simple, "Yes."

Even that was difficult to muster, the word slurring from my mouth.

Roxy was sitting bolt upright with a look of trepidation in her eyes.

"We've managed to stop the bleeding on her brain. She's on a ventilator at present. The next forty-eight hours are crucial. That's all I can tell you at the moment, I'm afraid."

The doctor was about to turn and walk away.

"She's going to be okay though, right?" queried Roxy.

The doctor nibbled at her bottom lip hesitantly, "We'll know more in a couple of days."

"Can we see her?" I begged.

The doctor seemed reluctant, but the desperation on our faces changed her mind. "Just for a few minutes."

Connie's slight frame lay shrouded by white linen. Machines hovered around her bed like mechanical guards, beeping and flashing rhythmically. Invasive tubes tethered her body in position. Her head was heavily bandaged, her eyes a rainbow of purples and blues. Her skin was pallid, and waxy to the touch.

I held her hand and closed my eyes, searching for a remnant of her, a spiritual sign that she was still in there, but she gave me nothing. Perhaps she was in between worlds, the physical and the spiritual, still uncertain of which one to pick.

"You getting anything?" sobbed Roxy. I shook my head despondently.

"If anyone can get through this, it's Connie," consoled Marie, who was hovering in the doorway.

We could only wait and hope that she was right.

CHAPTER TWENTY-SIX

It had been a few days since Connie's attack, and the police had many questions, most of which I could not answer without finding myself in a straitjacket.

Connie had made no further progress, though she was labeled 'stable.' The medics were scratching their heads; all of her vitals were normal, but Connie was still unconscious.

"This case is quite an enigma," I'd heard the specialist relay to his juniors, "everything about the patient appears normal, and yet she remains comatose." He walked away, shaking his head with a posse of white coats hanging on his every word.

Each day, Roxy and I visited the hospital after work, playing Connie her favorite music and reading books by her preferred authors. The room was alive with flowers and get-well wishes.

"I hadn't realized you were so popular, Con," giggled Roxy, overwhelmed by the colors and aromas from her many bouquets.

"This one's from Reggie," I informed, reading the requisite attached card.

Marie and a few of our neighbors had brought food baskets and offers of hot meals. We scheduled our lives between work and the hospital with little time for anything else.

I prayed for a sign that my friend still lived within the confines of her paralyzed existence, though I feared she may not. Sonia made a brief appearance, bringing me a dated photograph of Baxter Hempell's surrogate father.

"It's all I could find," she explained apologetically.

The detail was vague, but the picture had made it to the front page of the Sweet Water Tribune. Baxter and Cora Hempell in the foreground had been snapped outside their home a couple of days after their son's disappearance. Standing in the background, desperate to avoid the camera, was the figure of another man. I stared at the grainy image. Something about the face was familiar.

"You recognize him, Leni?" Sonia enquired enthusiastically.

"I feel like I've seen his face before, but... wait!" Reaching for my purse, I delved inside to retrieve the framed photograph from Erasmus Cobb's bedroom.

The images matched. The face of the man standing beside Erasmus was the same as the face in the newspaper.

"Erasmus and Mahru Iwuagwu (or Mr Moon, for ease of pronunciation) knew each other," I revealed excitedly.

"Maybe another trip to St. Bernadette's is in order. Sonia, you can come with me this time."

The following Saturday, as Roxy headed to the hospital, I drove to Sonia's colonial-style home on the outskirts of Crowther's Beach.

Eric was there, his car sitting beside his sister's in the driveway. I pulled alongside and checked my face in the sideview mirror.

Sonia was bursting with enthusiasm, "I've so much to tell you, Leni. Make yourself comfortable."

Eric gestured I should sit on the chair beside him. Of course, I wasn't going to argue.

"Firstly, here's a little something for Connie," Sonia handed me a colorful gift bag. I could tell in an instant that the contents were books and magazines.

"Secondly, Eric has managed to pull the blueprints for the Hempell's original house."

Eric on cue spread the plans across the table. He pointed out the extra room we had stumbled upon and its connection to the basement, both alterations being made at the hands of the then owners, the Hempells.

"Interesting, though we still have no idea what that room was used for. That stone table certainly looked purpose-built, reminded me of an altar," I proffered.

"Like in a church?" queried Sonia.

"Kinda, but cruder than that, more befitting to sacrifice, I guess."

"Absolutely," agreed Eric, "the hole in the center allows blood to drain into the bucket below."

"Sounds gruesome," added Sonia, "what would they be sacrificing, animals?"

"Or children," Eric and I replied in chorus.

"Oh, my goodness. I never thought of that, how awful."

"We don't have any evidence of that yet, but there was a ceremonial dagger kept there, and I'd hazard a guess that the markings on the floor were some kind of witchcraft."

"Voodoo," corrected Eric.

"Voodoo—that's a kind of African witchcraft, isn't it? How do you know it's voodoo?" I quizzed.

"I took photos on my cell phone and checked them out. It's definitely voodoo, and that doll we found with Victoria's face on it, just another confirmation."

"So, we're dealing with some kind of ritual killings?"

"Could be," agreed Eric.

The room fell silent for a moment as we processed the disturbing information. Was it possible that children were being slaughtered in suburbia?

"Eric also made another discovery," added Sonia, breaking the silence.

"I'm a bit of an amateur astronomer," he began, "a kinda hobby. Living beside the ocean, I get great views of the sky at night."

For a moment, I was transported to Eric's balcony, sipping cocktails as he surveyed the stars beside me.

I shook the thought away before the palpitations began.

"I was looking at the dates of the abductions, looking for a sort of pattern, I suppose. Then it hit me; I went through the dates one by one, and I realized..."

My cell phone buzzed loudly. It was Roxy. My heart skipped a beat.

"She's awake," bellowed her excited voice. "She's okay."

The relief was overwhelming, I grabbed my bag and rushed towards the door.

"Sorry, guys—Connie's woke up. I really need to go see her."

Chapter Twenty-Seven

Connie was sitting in bed eating grapes and chocolates.

"Want one?" she offered as I rushed into the room, a huge Connie smile crossing her lips.

"Of course I do, thought you'd never ask?"

"I can come home in a couple of days," she said.

"Shame, we've rented out your room," joked Roxy.

Connie laughed and talked and talked and talked, until she tired herself out.

"So good to have her back, isn't it, Leni?"

"Sure is. The house has been so quiet without her."

A couple of days later, Connie was back home as if nothing had happened. She seemed relatively unaffected by her traumatic ordeal save for the disfiguring scar carved into the left side of her scalp.

She remembered nothing of that night—the man in the top hat or the brutality of his cane. The police closed her case through lack of evidence and Connie's amnesia.

"Do you think she's really okay or just putting on a brave face?" I asked Roxy when Connie was taking an afternoon nap.

"Seems like the old Connie to me, why?"

"Oh, no reason. Just wondering, that's all."

When life was beginning to resemble something close to normal, I was awoken from sleep by the sound of a woman screaming.

The voice was familiar. I listened intently, realizing it belonged to Marie Richards.

From my bedroom window, I could see Marie pacing the sidewalk barefoot. Her screams were indescribable; she sounded immensely distraught.

I grabbed a robe and sped outside.

"Marie, are you okay?" I shouted, holding my robe tightly against the chill of the evening breeze.

Marie headed towards me and grabbed my shoulders, her tiny body shivering uncontrollably against mine.

"It's Victoria. She's missing!" she shrieked.

"What do you mean missing?"

"She's not in her room; her bed is empty," she cried.

"Have you checked everywhere else in the house, the backyard?"

"Yes, yes, but she's nowhere to be found." Marie crumpled to the ground, sobbing hysterically.

I shook her into reality and pulled her upwards, tucking my arm around her, and led her home.

Tate was in the hallway. Sheer panic framed his face. I threw him a questioning "Anything?"

He shook his head.

"Have you called 911?"

Tate nodded. I positioned Marie on the sofa and tossed a blanket round her icy frame.

"Have you checked everywhere?" I questioned, walking Tate out of earshot.

"Everywhere I can think of," he replied, his eyes pooling with tears.

"Okay, now go keep your mom company until the police arrive. I'm going to take a look around myself."

As Tate turned to obey my request, I caught hold of his arm, "Has everything been okay here? Nothing weird like before?"

Tate didn't need to speak. The answer was in his expression.

Just as I feared, the entity that possessed the Richards' house had never left. The cleansing had been too easy.

It was clever and cunning. It's unthreatening behavior towards Father Yakub a façade to trick the Richards into returning home. It lusted for Victoria, and now she was missing. It was eerily quiet as I swept the house for signs of the little girl, but I was aware of the evil all around me, lurking in the shadows, a malign disease waiting to unleash its misery upon this fragile, broken family.

The troubled spirits of children crossed my path, their presence chilling the air around me. They bore the same disfigurement as Jimmy Kale, their identities unquestionable. I spied the little boy in the midst of his peers, illuminated by the glow of a full moon. He pointed upwards, his finger stretching towards the skylight and the radiant globe that hovered there.

I followed his direction, "Don't wake the moon," resounding in my head. But what did it mean?

Suddenly, his small body rose upwards, hovering high in the air, his arms and legs dangling loosely, his head forced backwards as his whole body began shaking violently. He was whipped from side to side, dancing like a disjointed marionette, his puppet master disguised in the shadows. Just as quickly, he was discarded, and in one swift action was hurled violently across the room towards the moonlit window. My instinct was to scream as I waited for the sound of his small body hitting the glass, but there was no sound, no breaking glass. Jimmy Kale had disappeared.

I raced down the staircase towards the disdainful secret room in the basement, but the door wouldn't open, holding firm against my intention.

The voices of law enforcement echoed in the distance as two officers approached. "You okay, ma'am? We heard you scream."

"Yes, thank you. I'm fine—thought I saw something, scared myself, is all," I explained timidly.

As the police vehicles pulled away, I headed home with Marie and Tate beside me.

The next morning, Connie and Roxy made missing posters of Victoria and displayed them around the neighborhood. The task was futile; Victoria's disappearance was the work of something otherworldly, but my girlfriends yearned to help.

"That's usually what people do when someone goes missing," Roxy had argued.

Search parties assembled outside the Richards' house as news of the missing girl circulated. Surrounding areas were combed as shocked neighbors, police officers, and sniffer dogs searched for Victoria.

"Do you think it's happening again?" I heard one woman ask her husband.

"I pray to God it isn't," came his reply.

Sweet Water Bay housed a large church-going community. The existence of devil worship, voodooism, and human sacrifice was something its occupants only ever witnessed in movies. These god-fearing folk would never accept that a child had been abducted by someone or something other than a member of their community, and so the charade of searching for Victoria continued.

I joined the search like a good neighbor, combing the manicured gardens of Bittersweet Avenue, though I knew in my heart the task was fruitless.

Sonia and Eric arrived to offer their help. I put them to work in my kitchen, supplying hot drinks and sandwiches to weary volunteers.

As daylight disappeared into darkness, the community dispersed, tired and deflated. Victoria Richards was still missing.

In the warmth of the kitchen, we dined: Roxy, Connie, Eric, Sonia, Marie, Tate, and me. Marie picked at her food but ate nothing, excusing herself and retiring to bed.

"Where do you think the girl is?" quizzed Eric after Marie had left the room.

"I have my own theory, but you'd think me crazy if I told you."

Eric looked intrigued, "Try me," he wagered.

I hesitated. It was one thing to express my thoughts with Connie and Roxy, but Eric would surely run a mile if I started talking about ghosts and gremlins.

"She thinks the thing that lives in our house has got her," interrupted Tate, "don't you?"

The room silenced as everyone looked towards me.

"I told you. I don't believe in ghosts," snorted Eric.

"No, but you were shit scared down in that basement, admit it," I couldn't help myself. Eric's face flushed slightly. He didn't reply.

"Eric is a skeptic," added Sonia.

"Even though you yourself have a gift?" I shot Sonia a disapproving look.

"Okay, okay, I don't believe in ghosts and spirits and all the things you and Sonia presume to make contact with, but that room was real, the table was real, the knife was real, the... Eric stopped himself before revealing to Tate the image of his sister found on the head of a voodoo doll.

Too late, Tate was engaged in the conversation, "What room with a table and a knife?"

Eric looked at me and shrugged.

"Keep this to yourself, Tate, but there's a kind of add-on beyond the laundry room accessed through a small tunnel. You wouldn't know it existed. It sits between the level of the kitchen and the basement. We found a sacrificial table and an altar. It must have belonged to the Hempells."

"Is that where Victoria is?" Tate became agitated. "We need to go back to the house and check."

Eric grabbed the boy's arm abruptly as he rose from the table, "It's not safe right now, wait until the morning. Besides, the police have probably already found it, and if Victoria was there, we would have been informed."

I knew the police would never find it, and so did Eric. We just happened upon it in our quest to escape, but for now Tate seemed satisfied.

"Promise me, Tate, you won't go there alone?" I pleaded.

When Tate had retired to bed, I revealed my encounter with Jimmy Kale. I expected Eric to have a sarcastic comment, but instead he sat with his mouth slightly open, and his eyes hypnotized by my words.

"Are you okay, Eric?" I questioned. "You look like you've seen a ghost."

"Not a ghost," replied Eric, "but what you just said about him pointing at the moon; it was a full moon, right?"

"Er... yes, it was."

"Remember when you visited Sonia's a couple of weeks ago, and I was just about to tell you something when Roxy rang to say Connie was awake?"

"Yes?"

"I was going to tell you that all the children disappeared on dates when there was a full moon."

For a moment, it was difficult to process Eric's words.

"Don't wake the moon! That was written on my bathroom mirror," I revealed.

"But what does it mean?" queried Roxy.

"I'm not sure, but I know it's relevant to those children. Jimmy Kale knows, and he's trying to tell me."

"Wait a minute," started Sonia, a spark of realization twinkling behind her glasses, "Hempell was adopted by an African man..."

"Yes, Mahru Iwuagwu?"

"Well, Mahru—or Mr Moon as we've named him—practiced voodoo. Turns out he's wanted in Africa in connection with a number of child disappearances."

"When did you find that out?" I questioned.

"A couple of days ago but, with Victoria missing there just wasn't a good time to bring it up," explained Sonia.

"Eric, can you contact the authorities in Africa and find out more about our 'Mr Moon'?"

Eric nodded.

"Sonia, tomorrow, you and I have a date with Erasmus Cobb."

Chapter Twenty-Eight

Victoria had been missing for forty-eight hours, and the police were no closer to offering an explanation. Marie was devastated. Chase's suicide, the house of horrors she called home, and now her missing daughter combined to push her towards breaking point.

I sat alone, trawling through work emails, though their contents held little interest. My mind was too preoccupied with the events of the last few days.

I typed Victoria Richards' name into my browser, and in an instant the image of the cute little girl filled the screen. Her mischievous smile, the fiendish glint in her formidable blue eyes, and the hint of a dimple in her right cheek.

I closed my eyes and focused intensely on her image, searching the parameters of my spiritual psyche. I was desperate for a glimmer of inspiration, a shred of something to confirm she was still amongst the living. Deep in the recesses of that world between worlds, where the dead wait patiently for the light to welcome them home, I hunted. Thankfully, Victoria was not there.

It was time to depart the shadows and resume my place with the living, but I couldn't get back. A powerful force encompassed me, holding me steadfast in the cavernous void between the living and the dead.

Panic rose within me as I struggled to cross dimensions. A sudden firm grip tugged at my hand. Blinded by darkness, I floated uncontrollably through the realm of the dead.

A moment later, I was standing in a room, that secret room, in the Richards' basement.

A man was hovering beside the stone table, his head bowed from view. He was chanting repetitively and brandishing a dagger. He threw his head back, the brim of his top hat visible in the candlelight. His face was garnished in white paint, the outline of a skull decorating his complexion. His eyes glowed intensely, a fiery red, and his chanting intensified as he thrust the dagger deep into the bare flesh of a young child. Blood poured instantly into the metal bucket below as the man thrust again.

At that moment, another man entered the room clad in a gray robe. The oversized hood hid his face, but the skin of his hands was pale. He was carrying a glass jar filled with dark liquid that he held above the stone table. The man in the top hat opened his mouth, a momentary flash of needle-sharp teeth plunged forward, ripping into the body of the child, tearing away its tongue, its heart, and finally its eyes. One by one, he spat the organs into the glass jar, churning the liquid momentarily. He nodded to the man in the robe, who instantly placed the jar on the altar. Producing a ball of thick black yarn and a large needle from beneath his robe, he approached the blood-soaked body of the child and proceeded to pierce the child's lips, sewing crudely across the tiny mouth.

I wrestled to free myself from the horrors of that room. I had seen too much. I wanted to scream but found no voice. The man in the top hat smirked, as if he knew I was there, watching. Blood streaked his jacket and sprayed from his mouth as he licked at the remnants with a forked tongue. He left the room as the other man tossed the child's body from the table to a sackcloth below and hauled the small bundle down the stairs towards the basement.

I recognized the child as he lay drowning in his own blood. I had witnessed the brutal massacre of Jimmy Kale, watching helplessly as his young life was extinguished.

I struggled again and this time I was free, falling through the darkness and finding softness on a mountain of pillows, as I landed safely on my bed.

Had the whole disturbing incident simply been a nightmare? Had I dreamt the whole experience? I was confused. The answer was there in a smear of red blood on the bed sheets, where the soles of my feet had stained the white linen, and I knew in that moment it was real.

Chapter Twenty-Nine

I met Sonia in the parking lot of St. Bernadette's having requested a second visit with the inimitable Barbara, introducing Sonia as my younger sister.

Barbara repeated her whirlwind tour for Sonia's benefit, then ushered us towards the exit.

"I'm not ready to leave just yet," announced an irritated Sonia.

Barbara smoothed the pleats of her plaid skirt, struggling to maintain her composure.

"I'm afraid there's nothing more to see. The tour is over."

"I would like to speak to some of your residents, get a feel for the place from their perspective," requested Sonia.

"That's not possible; our residents cannot be disturbed," Barbara replied.

"What about Erasmus Cobb? You allowed Leni to visit with him, didn't you?"

Barbara flushed with color, clearly exasperated by Sonia's persistence. "Five minutes, that's all I will allow. You know where to find him."

"Thanks—five minutes is all I need," revealed Sonia.

"What were you going to do if she said no?" I queried as we crossed the corridor to the old man's room.

"No idea. I hadn't thought that far in advance," giggled Sonia.

"Now, brace yourself. This isn't going to be pleasant," I warned, opening the door to Erasmus's room.

Sonia covered her nose, "Oh my God! You're not wrong about the smell, Leni; it's incredibly strong."

Erasmus lay in bed just where I had left him a few days earlier, but this time his eyes were open.

I pulled back the drapes, flooding the room with daylight and revealing the source of the horrendous stench. Erasmus Cobb lay half-naked in urine-soaked sheets, and the stains of human excrement decorated the space around him.

"Holy shit!" exclaimed Sonia. "Should I go get someone to clean him up?"

"Later—let's get what we came for first."

The emaciated carcass in the bed shielded his eyes from the brightness.

"Who are you?" he growled, glancing at me then Sonia.

"We're detectives, Erasmus, here to ask you some questions," I asserted.

"About what?"

"About this man," I held the framed photograph in front of him.

He squinted at the image, screwing up his face with disdain.

"That's you, isn't it?" I questioned, pointing at the younger version of himself.

"Might be."

"Don't worry, Mr Cobb. "We're not interested in you and what you might or might not have done with your life, but we do need to know who your friend is."

"I've served my time, repented my sins, shan't be here much longer, I hope."

"That's as maybe, so it won't hurt for you to tell us who your friend is," I reiterated.

"Why, what's he done?"

"That's not your concern. Just tell us who he is, and we will leave you alone."

Erasmus grabbed the photo from my hand and held it close. Gray eyes tinged with yellow stared into the image like it was the first time he had seen it. A bony finger stabbed at the glass as a wiry grin crossed his lips. The spark of recognition ignited his shriveled features, and he chuckled fiendishly.

"That's my mate," he declared. "Haven't seen him for years."

"What's his name? Can you remember?"

"Some long-winded foreign sounding thing; I could never say it right. Ended up calling him Mr Moon for ease."

Sonia glanced towards me with anticipation.

"Mr Moon. Why did you call him that?"

"That's what he told me to call him, why d'ya think?" Erasmus scowled.

"Okay, so he called himself Mr Moon. But how did you meet him?"

The old man pondered for a while as if the question had overheated his aging brain. Finally, he said, "We was cellmates."

Chapter Thirty

The following morning, I faked illness and waited for the house to empty. In the safety of solitude, I made my way to the Richards' house and slipped inside.

The gruesome events that had played out a couple of days earlier still haunted me, and I was desperate to check the murderous room beneath the Richards' house.

Victoria was still missing, and I had to be certain that she wasn't being kept there or worse still was the next victim of ritual slaughter.

The laundry room door was no longer stuck and opened with ease, allowing me entry. I lowered myself into the tunnel and crawled nervously along its splintered length.

The air inside the claustrophobic passageway was freezing though summer temperatures raged outside. The warmth of my breath brushed pleasantly against my face as I pushed through the darkness.

Suddenly, I was not alone. Something was following behind me. I could smell its malevolent presence, feel its toxicity growing stronger. I fumbled through the darkness, panic in every movement, fear ravaging my body like a malignant plague, hand outstretched, searching for the exit.

A moment later, I toppled out of the tunnel onto the hard, wooden floor of the secret room. Flashing the light of my cell into the darkness, hardly daring to breathe, I waited to confront the unwelcome companion that had followed behind me. But nothing appeared.

I stumbled to my feet, relieved by the solitude, and felt for the torch I had stored in my back pocket. The beam of light flashed across the room. It was much the same as the last time: the metal bucket was empty, only dry remnants of sanguine residue hard and crusty clung to the inside. The dagger still lay in its wooden coffin, bearing no evidence of recent use, but the doll bearing Victoria's face was gone.

I found the staircase leading to the basement and headed into the bowels of the house. At first glance it was a standard basement, housing a myriad of discarded objects, collectibles, and the obligatory furnace. Racks of discarded paint tins and bags of clothing lined one wall. I tugged at the contents of a bag, sending an avalanche of clothing spewing at my feet.

In the glow of torchlight, the items appeared small. Child-sized. I pulled a jacket from the pile, and a rough, green tweed material scratched at my fingers. Suddenly, the image of a boy was flashing through my head; he was crying uncontrollably as he was being dragged upstairs to meet his fate on the stone table. The bags were filled with clothing worn by the missing children, shoes, and soft toys hidden in the jumble of girls' dresses and boys' shorts.

A noise caught my attention, a shuffling sound behind me. I turned slowly, searching the shadows, torchlight bouncing erratically. The shuffling grew louder and closer, and the torch began to flicker, its light diminishing, plunging me into blackness. I rattled it frantically; it awoke with a momentary flash and lived just long enough to illuminate the tortured faces of small children staggering towards me.

They stood before me, an army of lost souls, devoid of sight and speech, all bearing the same afflictions as Jimmy Kale. I stumbled backwards, dropping the torch, and I heard it roll away into the shadows. Blinded by the darkness, I felt vulnerable and alone. My breathing shallowed, my heartbeat devoured by overwhelming fear, I stood rigid, frozen. I was afraid.

In the depth of my terror, a child's hand grasped mine. I knew instantly it was Jimmy Kale.

I could feel the tortured souls of the slaughtered children closing around me. Each had met their fate in the bowels of this house, hidden within its depth for decades, lost and forgotten.

Suddenly, the hand was gone, slipping through my fingers with a sense of urgency. The children were gone too—only the darkness remained.

Something was moving in the gloom of the basement, something sinister, something horrifying. A blood-curdling scream filled the space around me, piercing the air with the sharpness of a thousand daggers. A tornado of objects was swirling, licking my body like the tip of a whip, dancing around me and gathering speed. I dived to the ground, avoiding a multitude of items as they crashed around me.

Through the chaos of the storm, red, glowing eyes pulsed in the distance. I rolled into a ball and prayed.

It took a moment to realize that the room had fallen silent, and I opened my eyes cautiously, fearful of what I might find. But in the calmness after the storm, I saw only Noni, standing like an angel, enveloped in warm light.

I wanted to run to her, hug like we used to, tell her how much I missed her. I started towards her with tears cascading down my cheeks, but Noni stepped backwards on my approach. She pointed in the direction of a small window, and when I looked back, she was gone.

Her message was clear: she wanted me to leave the house. The small window had been my escape once before. I didn't hesitate. I pulled myself through the opening and out into the fresh summer air.

Chapter Thirty-One

In a remote corner of Nigeria on a cool October morning, Akin Adebowale pushed his way into the world, heralding his existence with tumultuous cries.

His mother was no stranger to the birthing process, Akin being her tenth delivery in as many years. She reached forward, lifting the baby onto her breast and staring at the new life she had expelled from her womb. But as she gazed upon the baby boy, her eyes widened, and her face creased with panic. She called for her husband.

He stooped above the layers of linen swaddling the newborn, spying the fuzz of curly, yellow hair that poked into view. Curious, he pulled the fabric aside and stared in disbelief at the pale white skin of the child beneath. He gasped, shook his head, and ran from the birthing hut to the neighboring village two miles away.

He returned with the village elder and the witch doctor. One look at the child's appearance sent the witch doctor into bursts of repetitive chanting, dancing around the mother and child hysterically, shaking bones and hexes at the sleeping infant. The boy was considered a curse upon the village. His yellow hair and pallid skin would bring nothing but bad luck. The child could not be raised amongst them.

Akin was taken from his mother's arms and left many miles away from the village. Abandoned in the wilderness, it was hoped that he would not survive the night, instead falling prey to the drop in temperature or a hungry predator.

The following morning, he was gone. Snatched in the darkness by a nulliparous voodoo priestess who seemed unperturbed by the boy's appearance. She vowed to raise the child as her own. But Akin lived a solitary existence, beaten and abused by his surrogate mother, starved of nutrition, and living in perpetual fear of the woman who called herself Maman Kalfi.

She used his appearance to empower herself in the eyes of the villagers and taught him voodoo practice, using sacrifice to appease the Gods.

To Akin, the rituals of voodooism became part of normal life, whether it was a chicken laid across the altar—or a child he was taught it was a necessary sacrifice. He knew he would never meet the same fate. His anemic skin tone and bright blue eyes were of no interest to the gods; the priestess had made that clear on many occasions.

As Akin entered his tenth year, the priestess fell ill and died, leaving him alone once again. The villagers drove him away after the new priestess showed no interest in him.

He wandered across Nigeria in search of the parents Maman Kalfi said had abandoned him, but his parents had both lost their lives to Ebola when an outbreak had ravaged their village.

Akin learned of a man named Mahru Iwuagwu, who was possibly his grandfather, though the fact was questionable.

Akin chose to believe that the man was related and found him living a remote, nomadic lifestyle on the outskirts of his birth village.

The man, Mahru, readily accepted Akin into his home. He had heard tales of the white boy with yellow hair and blue eyes, who resided with a powerful priestess, and Mahru longed to inherit her knowledge. He relished the chance to acquire her teachings, knowing that the boy had been privy to her powers.

It wasn't long before Mahru had convinced the boy to serve him as he had the priestess. The innocence of his youth and the relief Akin had felt at finding a member of his family made him the perfect partner. He did not question his grandfather when asked to abduct small children for sacrifice, but Akin failed to realize that, unlike the priestess, Mahru was a psychotic sociopath with a thirst for the blood of the young and innocent.

They lived together in a small house just outside Abuja, the capital city. It was here that Akin enticed unsuspecting victims, and Mahru conducted ritualistic sacrifice, which always included removal of the eyes and the tongue, as well as the stitching together of the lips with thick black twine.

As Akin entered puberty, Mahru took him to America. The reason was given that he wanted Akin to receive education, but the truth was that Mahru was a wanted man, and the net was closing in on his capture. Unbeknown to Akin, the man who posed as his grandfather was wanted in connection with the abduction and possible murder of more than thirty children across Nigeria.

They settled in New York, in an apartment block for immigrants, and Akin received tutoring at the local community center. It soon became apparent that the Nigerian boy was intelligent, excelling at every subject and passing every examination with top grades.

Akin was accepted into university, where he met Cora Hempell and fell in love. Mahru found himself suddenly demoted in Akin's list of priorities as Cora became the main focus of his attention.

As Akin's life and love grew more successful, he asked Cora for her hand in marriage. He changed his name, taking Hempell as his surname and using Baxter, the nickname she had given him when they first met.

The couple began married life in a simple home, which Mahru funded in return for a room. As Baxter's writings grew in popularity, so too did his bank account, and a year later—just before the birth of their son—they moved into Bittersweet Avenue. Mahru's money was no longer needed, and he fell even further down Baxter's priority list. For that reason, he detested the newly-born Byron.

Mahru pleaded with Cora's good nature and moved into the new house with them, a decision Baxter would soon come to regret.

One evening as Cora carried their son to bed, Mahru took his opportunity to change the house rules and bestow upon Baxter the disturbing facts of his past.

"You know, Akin, she loves that boy so much," Mahru declared.

"Yes, we both do, grandfather. My name is not Akin now; it's Baxter. Why must you insist on addressing me that way when I constantly remind you that Akin no longer exists?" Baxter fumed.

Mahru paid no mind to his grandson's words, "Imagine how horrified Cora would be to discover your past."

Baxter was caught off guard, "Whatever do you mean?" he questioned.

"Come now, Akin, you lured boys like Byron back to our house, where you watched me kill and mutilate them," sniggered Mahru.

"In the name of the gods," Baxter protested.

"You really aren't that clever, are you?" snarled Mahru. "You honestly believe that was the real reason I did those things?"

Baxter shuffled uncomfortably in his chair, flashbacks of the children and his grandfather's actions racing through his mind. He rose from the table, stumbling backwards in an effort to distance himself from the monster who sat in his family's kitchen.

Mahru growled, "How stupid are you, Akin? You really believed everything I told you, didn't you?"

"Get out of my house! You disgust me," cried Baxter, but Mahru sat firm.

"I will tell Cora everything, right here, right now. She will never allow you near that child again."

Baxter dithered by the back door, he was desperate to turn the handle and remove Mahru from his life forever. If Cora were to discover the despicable acts of his younger years, whether committed naively or not, she would never forgive him. His grip softened, and he regained his seat at the table.

"Now, listen to me," dictated Mahru. "Cora remains unaware, provided you follow my rules."

It was on that day that life in the Hempell house changed completely.

Chapter Thirty-Two

The fragments of information we had collected were coming together like pieces of a jigsaw puzzle, though the most significant pieces were still missing. Eric had dug out scant information on Mr Moon and his relationship with Erasmus Cobb. They had shared a cell in the local penitentiary, Cobb for possessing indecent images of children and attempted abduction, but Moon's file was conveniently missing, leaving nothing more than speculation about his imprisonment.

Eric had set up an interview with Wade Koblenzsky, the warden, for the following day.

I was frustrated, torn between the hunt for Victoria and my desire to solve the case of the missing children, which definitely had something to do with the Richards' house.

Marie had disappeared into a world of Xanax and diazepam, spending most days in bed. Tate, feeling abandoned by his distraught mother, spent his days moping around the house in his boxers and headphones. His schoolwork was neglected, and his attendance nonexistent.

The police investigation had slowed. I was drowning in despondency.

And then, that evening as I hauled my weary, disappointed self to bed, a call came in from Sonia. She sounded breathless and agitated, almost hysterical.

"Sonia, calm down. You're not making any sense," I pleaded.

"Leni, I've just had the strangest dream," she began, "I must have nodded off during an episode of Red Herring… it was just so real: I saw her, I heard her cries, I was digging at the earth, desperate to find her. Leni, it was Victoria. I think I know where she is."

Sonia sounded exhausted as she sobbed with relief.

"Describe everything in detail," I pleaded, "leave nothing out."

Sonia's dream, premonition, call it what you will, took her into a woodland setting, where she was guided by the cries of a distraught child. The deeper she went, the louder the cries became until she was standing beside a dilapidated wooden structure that had once resembled a type of shed. The door to the building was hanging by one hinge and moving slowly in the wind. Inside, there was a mound of freshly turned earth, and the faintest tapping sound between the creaks and moans of the old outbuilding could be heard from beneath the ground. Sonia had fallen to her knees at this point and started scraping at the soil, her fingers digging frantically as she clawed through the earth to free the child trapped below. And then she woke up.

Sleep was incomprehensible that night as I tossed Sonia's words around repeatedly. I could hardly wait for dawn to break before I marched in the direction of the Richards' backyard. The expanse of lawned area behind their house flowed into a vast wooded area beyond.

Sweet Water Bay was known for its coastline and sandy beaches, but it also hosted a maze of forest areas, the remnants untouched by settlers decades earlier.

The undergrowth grew deeper with every footstep away from civilization, and the light dimmed beneath the canopy of overgrown plane trees as the early morning sunshine struggled to make an appearance. I wasn't on familiar territory. In fact, I hadn't ventured into this area since I was a young girl playing hide and go seek with Annie and her brother Chuck, who lived in the house on the other side of Noni's. Everything had changed; mother nature's maturing spell had transformed it, but it was a place I was drawn to in my search for Victoria, and the details of Sonia's dream seemed to point me in its direction.

I was thinking of turning back as brambles tugged at the hem of my jeans, piercing my ankles with needle-sharp thorns. I heard a rustling behind as the undergrowth swayed with movement. I froze as the bracken parted and the bushy tail of a raccoon brushed the air above. I smiled with relief, losing my footing and falling headlong onto the dewy floor beneath. A brace of grouse took flight around me, startled from the cover of thicket. The noise was deafening, but in the aftermath of silence, I spotted the remnants of a wooden structure in the distance.

Brushing forest debris from my clothing, I headed towards the ramshackle building. It wore a coat of green moss and was slowly disappearing beneath a plethora of ivy. The forest was holding it precariously in position; one false tug at the vine and the whole lot was likely to crumble into nothing. I ventured closer, now able to see the remains of a door hanging delicately from one hinge. I recalled Sonia's description; this must be the place she had seen in her dream.

I debated my uneasiness, but I couldn't turn back now. If this was the place, then Victoria could be inside.

With a slow and cautious movement, I managed to ease beyond the disjointed entrance.

Inside, the rafters above had all but succumbed to the weathering of time, held in part by the wandering branches of a nearby oak and the invasion of interwoven creepers.

The floor was in much better condition, splintered and rotten around the edge but firm underfoot with the remnant of a faded rug covering its center.

My eyes were drawn to the mutilated tassels of the woven matting as they tickled a fresh layer of earth. I whipped the patch of carpet backwards, uncovering a rectangular impression in the soil beneath.

"Victoria," I shouted, waiting and listening for a reply, but none came.

I forced a plank of wood free and began scraping. At first, there was nothing but soil, and then the sound of wood hitting wood stopped me in my tracks. I'd hit a trapdoor. Brushing a final layer of soil aside, I fumbled with a rusted metal ring. Pulling with everything I had, the ground opened beneath me, and I was peering into the darkness below.

"Victoria," my voice echoed through the cavity, and I waited.

Suddenly, somewhere in the distance, the faintest voice called back. Could it be Victoria, or was I being lured into a deadly trap? No one knew where I was; I risked being incarcerated, lost forever, but if Victoria was down there, I had the chance to rescue her.

My heart overruled my head, and before I knew it, I was descending stone steps and disappearing into the darkness.

The light of my cell phone was my only guide as I entered what resembled a large tunnel. It was possibly the remnants of an old mine, but, to my knowledge, Sweet Water Bay was not an accomplished mining town. I followed the propped walls and vaulted ceiling, stopping sporadically to check the space around me. Fortunately, the tunnel only traveled in one direction, and after ten minutes, I still hadn't reached the end. Panic descended, a second thought. Should I turn back?

"Victoria!" I screamed into the emptiness. A child's voice answered.

Jogging through the tunnel now, I kept calling out until the response grew louder. I was nearing the source.

Then, in front of me, a solid wooden door halted my journey. I banged against it with my shoulder, but I was no match for its strength. I forced at the handle, but it was fruitless. If Victoria was on the other side, then this door was the only thing stopping me from saving her. What to do?

I stooped to the keyhole, flashing light through its tiny opening.

"Victoria, are you in there?"

"Yes." The voice was feeble and afraid.

"Can you come to the door for me?" I questioned.

"No," came the response.

"Why not?"

"I'm stuck."

"Okay, sweetheart. I'm going to get you out of there; don't worry," I soothed as the sound of frightened sobs radiated from the room beyond.

It was a long shot, a movie trick, but I had to try. Standing tall and reaching above the door frame my fingers searched in a desperate bid to find a key. I couldn't believe it as I nudged a small, solid object, knocking it to the floor. There in the dirt lay the answer to Victoria's freedom.

The room was cold and dank, filled with the odor of moist earth. The flick of a nearby switch, and the room burst into light. As my eyes adjusted to the brightness, I searched for her. A stack of empty dog cages lined one wall, and the sound of pitiful whimpers led me to the corner where Victoria Richards lay, curled submissively in the fetal position.

"Hey, Victoria. It's me, Leni," I whispered softly.

The little girl lifted her head slowly, eyes streaked with dirty tears as she recognized my voice.

"Leni, help me," she cried, moving towards the front of the cage, tiny fingers poking through the bars.

I unhooked the feeble latch and freed the child. She scurried forward into my arms.

Her tiny body was shaking against mine.

"You're freezing," I said, the icy touch of her hands sending shivers down my spine. She was clad in the pajamas she had disappeared in and nothing more. The cage was empty except for a small bowl of water and a half-eaten bag of chips.

"Come on, let's get you home to your mommy."

I knew the tunnel led back to the outside, but the crude, underground prison that had held Victoria Richards for the last six days presented an alternative route. Up a stone staircase was a makeshift door not much bigger in size than Victoria herself. I shoved against it's stiffness, and it swung away, allowing us to crawl through. To my surprise, we were now standing in the Richards' basement, a place I had already encountered on two occasions before. I remembered the whereabouts of the tiny window and headed for freedom.

Chapter Thirty-Three

I cannot describe the rapturous welcome we received as I placed Victoria back in the arms of her mother. Marie cried an ocean of tears at the sight of her little girl and hugged her like she would never let go again.

When the police arrived to question me, Victoria was bathed and fed, then played with her dolls as if the events of the last few days had already been forgotten.

Sadly, Eric was not one of the officers who attended, but I relayed the morning's adventure to his colleague who eagerly documented every word.

"You say it was your friend, Sonia, who told you where to find the little girl?" he queried.

"That's right," I paused, knowing that what I was about to say could possibly end with me leaving in a straitjacket, "she had a... dream..."

The officer's eyes widened, "A dream?"

"That's right. She described it to me in detail, and that's how I found Victoria."

The officer scratched the side of his nose with a pencil as he digested my words.

"Ma'am, with respect, you're telling me you found the child from the description of a dream your friend had?"

"It's not unusual for psychics to receive messages through dreams, officer."

"So, she's a psychic?"

"Yes, we both are."

The officer grimaced at the thought of his captain's reaction when this report landed on his desk.

"Did you lose a brother recently?" I quizzed.

The officer's jaw dropped as he answered the question with a hesitant, "Yes."

"A terrible car accident, wasn't it? He died instantly, but his family survived. A wife and two children."

"You could have read that in the local news," he scoffed, "don't you work for the Tribune?"

"I do indeed, but the Tribune never reported that his wife was pregnant at the time. A baby son also died that day."

The officer paled, realizing that the information I had imparted was only known to himself and his sister-in-law.

"You look like you could use a coffee, officer."

When Victoria entered the living room, she was carrying a doll and her favorite blue teddy bear. The officer, who referred to himself as Grayson, welcomed her warmly.

He asked to hold the blue teddy and proceeded to ask his questions through the medium of the bear.

Victoria responded well to this, seeing the interview as nothing more than a game.

"Where did you go when you went away, Victoria?"

"I went to a dungeon," she replied.

"Gosh, that sounds scary. Were you afraid?"

"Yes, it was cold and dark."

"Were there any other children in the dungeon?"

"Yes, there was a little boy; he held my hand when I cried."

Grayson cast me a questioning glance. I shook my head and shrugged.

"Do you know the little boy's name?" he continued.

"Yes, it was Jimmy."

A cold shiver coasted the length of my spine as the boy's name left Victoria's lips.

The officer glanced again, but I said nothing.

"Who took you to the dungeon, Victoria?"

"I think it was my mommy!"

A wave of shocked faces circled the room.

"Why do you think it was mommy?" queried Grayson, his eyes holding Marie captive as she shook her head in disbelief.

"Cos she smelled like mommy."

This time, the officer's questioning glance was directed towards Marie, who, agitated, was pacing the room with her arms folded defensively.

"Victoria, sweetheart, mommy didn't take you away. Tell the officer it wasn't me," pleaded a distraught Marie.

"But it was you, mommy," replied Victoria.

My mind was racing with a million questions. Could Marie have taken her own daughter? Was it possible? Her reaction had certainly been that of a mother in absolute distress. Was she just a great actress?

I couldn't hold back any longer, "Is this true, Marie? Did you take Victoria?"

"Of course not; how could you even think that?" snapped Marie, falling onto the sofa in a flood of tears.

The officer was upright now and heading in Marie's direction.

"I think it best if we continue this conversation back at the station," he commanded.

Victoria was crying too now, wrapping her tiny hands around Marie's arm.

"It's okay, baby," soothed Marie.

Tate appeared, wondering what all the commotion was about. He whisked Victoria into his arms and hugged her.

"What's going on?" he questioned, stroking his sister's hair with comforting dexterity.

"I'm being arrested," sobbed Marie.

"Arrested, but why? I don't understand?"

I tried to usher Tate from the room, but he refused to leave.

"Victoria has named your mother as her abductor," stated the officer.

"That's ridiculous," scoffed Tate. "Tell him, mom. It wasn't you."

"Yes, it was," chirped Victoria.

Tate stared at his little sister, "Mom would never do anything like that."

His eyes danced from Victoria to Marie, the police officer and then me.

"It can't be true, Victoria," he snarled, shaking the child aggressively until her eyes pooled once again. "Did you see the lady's face? Was it mom?" he demanded. Victoria began to cry, but Tate asked again, "Well, did you?"

Through the avalanche of tears, a distraught Victoria refused to answer.

It was the one question that really mattered, but Victoria said nothing more.

As the police car drove away, we were left stunned.

"What on earth is going on?" demanded Connie as she arrived home from work, "I've just seen Marie in the back of a police car."

It had been a long day and was an even longer night as we waited for news of Marie. Tate managed to comfort Victoria, and she slept in his room that night. Downstairs, the three of us debated the day's events with much needed large glasses of Italian wine.

"You don't think it was Marie, do you?" queried Roxy.

"Honestly, Rox, I don't know what to think. I'm too tired to think."

"It doesn't make any sense though, Leni. Why would Marie abduct her own child?" doubted Connie.

"Why does anyone do anything, Connie? Why does it need to make sense? People do odd things for all sorts of reasons; maybe Marie had hers," I replied.

"*If* she did it," added Roxy.

"Let's just see what tomorrow brings. I'm about ready to turn in," I said wearily.

As I secured the locks, turned out the lights, and climbed into bed, I knew that sleep would not come easy, despite my exhaustion.

What had started with a momentous triumph had ended with shock and disbelief.

I couldn't fathom why Victoria would name Marie if it wasn't true; no one could have predicted that. No one could have predicted what was to happen next either.

Chapter Thirty-Four

I wasn't sure whether sleep had found me that night. I just remember the sirens blasting outside my window and the cacophony of noise exploding in the street below.

Roxy and Connie had heard it too; I met them on the stairs in pajamas and robes, ready to investigate.

Mr Cunliffe in the house directly opposite was heading up the sidewalk, his eyes fixed on the scenario that was unravelling in the distance.

"What's going on, Charlie?" asked Roxy, quickening her pace to reach his side.

"Nothing good. I'm sure of that," came his reply.

Connie and I hurried behind as the chill of the night air nipped at our bare feet. Roxy stopped abruptly a few paces ahead of us and was looking upwards towards the Richards' house. Reaching her side, we made a shocking discovery.

"Oh, my God. Is that...?"

The words had scarcely left my lips before Connie confirmed, "Marie."

A multitude of first responders had gathered at the foot of the Richards' driveway, police, paramedics, and fire fighters all on standby as a crowd of onlookers stood hypnotized by the sight of a woman standing on the ledge of a third-floor window.

Even from that distance, I knew it was Marie, her blond hair flowing freely in the breeze. I rushed forwards, only to be stopped by a burly police officer's gloved hand.

"Please, sir, I know her," I begged.

"I'm sure you do, miss, but this is a very delicate situation. We're handling it," he replied sarcastically.

"But I know what this is about; at least let me talk to her."

"Can't do that, ma'am—we have a professional on the way. Now, please stand back."

I raced to the other side of the drive, shouting in desperation, "Marie, don't do this, please."

Marie turned to look at me, then just as quickly turned to look behind as if she were not alone.

She launched herself forward, arms wide, the sleeves of her gown billowing gracefully as she plunged to her death.

I sank to my knees in disbelief. Marie's body lay lifeless and mangled on the steps of her home.

I glanced back through the swell of tears at the open window as the shadow of the man in the top hat stepped out of view.

A hand suddenly hooked around my arm, pulling me upwards. Eric was holding me close, cradling my face as Marie's body was enclosed in black plastic.

Back at the house, Tate and Victoria had heard nothing of the disturbance that was about to change their lives forever.

They would awake to tragic news and the realization that they were now orphans.

I managed to convince the authorities to allow the children to stay with us until after Marie's funeral. In light of the situation and the trauma Victoria had already suffered, they had reluctantly agreed, but I knew it was only a matter of time before we had to say goodbye.

As dawn broke, all that remained of the previous night's events was the dried bloodstain on the front steps of the Richards' house and liberal remnants of police tape blowing carelessly across the lawn.

The outside world was oblivious to the disastrous reality that was about to grip the lives of the two children racing hungrily towards the kitchen. They fell through the doorway, laughing uncontrollably, then stopped abruptly at the somber faces greeting them.

"What's up?" asked Tate. "Where's mom?"

The conversation I was about to have was going to be the most difficult one of my entire life.

"Sit down. There's something I need to tell you."

Chapter Thirty-Five

I met Eric later that day for our scheduled interview with the warden, Wade Koblenzsky.

Wade was a mountain of a man, tall, broad, and muscular. His appearance was intimidating, his voice commanding, and his manner brusque. I detected signs of a military background: short haircut, bald eagle tattoo partially hidden beneath his pristine white shirt, and dog tags that hung around his neck.

"Come in, take a seat," he ordered. "How can I help you?"

Eric explained the reason for our visit and its significance to the missing children. Wade listened intently.

"I have a vague recollection of those children, and if memory serves, a local man was the prime suspect," stated Wade. "Wasn't he charged?"

"No, sir," Eric confirmed. "He was released. There was no evidence of his involvement at the time, but it is his grandfather who we are here to talk about."

"And that would be…?"

"Mahru Iwuagwu," declared Eric.

Koblenzsky tapped the desk with the tip of his pen, "Yes. Mahru. I remember him."

"What can you tell us about him?" I questioned.

The warden locked eyes on me and held my gaze like a military target. His stare was uncomfortable, almost violating, but I couldn't look away.

"He was an unusual character, but he did his time, and being unusual isn't a crime," he answered.

"Unusual in what way?" queried Eric, much to my relief.

"He had weird beliefs, unnerved the other inmates, that sort of thing."

"Could you elaborate on the weird beliefs… please?" I hesitated to capture his gaze, but it was impossible not to do so.

"He worshipped the moon, some voodoo shit. Whenever there was a full moon, he would freak out the other inmates. They christened him the boogeyman. I've even heard him called the Devil."

Eric glanced towards me for a reaction.

"You're not a believer, Mr Koblenzsky?" I enquired.

"In voodoo? Hell no. I believe in justice, in the law and in God, but I don't condemn a man because his belief is different from mine."

I wasn't about to enter into a debate on religion and changed the subject.

"He shared a cell with Erasmus Cobb," I continued.

"Yeah, Cobb was the only guy in here that would share with him," came the reply.

"How did they get on?"

Wade pondered for a moment, "I got the feeling they shared a common interest."

"And that would be what?"

"Children." The answer was blunt but informative.

"Cobb was serving time for possessing indecent images of children and attempted abduction; what was Mahru in for?"

"He was found guilty of grooming a minor and sentenced to serve two years."

Eric glanced again. This time, my reaction was one of surprise.

"Can you give us the name of the minor?" I pleaded.

"No, ma'am; the child was underage and remained anonymous throughout. Not even I am privy to that information."

Our visit with the warden had been helpful in that we learned of Mr Moon's interest in children, but interest and murder were a far cry from each other. We were no nearer to stamping 'guilty' on our prime suspect. The identity of his victim was key to our investigation, but how we obtained such information was yet another hurdle we had to overcome.

Chapter Thirty-Six

The house felt empty now. The Richards family had kept us occupied for many months, and the year was coming to a close with Christmas festivities just around the corner. I missed the kids; we all did. The day they drove away to separate foster homes was devastating.

Marie's funeral was our final day together before they were dragged from our lives and driven away in the back of a shiny, black Buick.

In part, life fell back into routine, and my focus returned to the missing children investigation. The Richards' house went up for sale but received little in the way of interest; not surprising I suppose, given its tragic history.

Tate texted constantly, deeply unhappy with his new foster family. He threatened to run away and begged incessantly for me to bring him home. I battled with the local authority, but all endeavors were fruitless. My age and lifestyle made me an unsuitable foster parent.

Victoria, it seemed, had settled comfortably with her new family, and communication from her was sporadic.

Sonia and I, with the occasional visit from Eric, resumed our weekly updates on the missing children. Progress was slow, enthusiasm had waned slightly, and Jimmy Kale had not appeared since Marie's death and Victoria's absence. The search for Mr Moon's grooming victim was both desperate and arduous.

Connie and Roxy partied hard, washing away memories in a sea of alcohol and recreational drugs.

Connie refused to open her bedroom curtains, living in constant fear of glimpsing the man in the top hat, who had brought so much misery into all our lives.

Roxy would leave the room at any mention of the Richards family; she simply couldn't bear to discuss them. It's fair to say we all dealt with the tragedy and loss in very different ways. On the eve of the holidays, a thick blanket of snow had fallen over Sweet Water Bay, the first in many years. The neighborhood twinkled to the colors of a million bright lights as homes and gardens had been decorated for the holiday season.

Connie, Roxy, and I had stayed home that day to prepare the house for a handful of invited guests that evening.

The tree was dressed, the yard decorated, eggnog and mulled wine prepared as the sound of happiness and excitement resonated temporarily throughout the house. The dulcet tones of Nat King Cole's little drummer boy resounded cheerfully as guests arrived and the party began.

The house buzzed with the sound of voices and laughter. Wine flowed, and music played. Roxy brought out the compulsory game of Twister when everyone was sufficiently inebriated to take part. I, as usual, was first to be knocked out—great balance, especially under the influence, not being my strong point. I retreated to the kitchen to fill up my glass. My cell buzzed; it was Tate again. I wanted to reply, but I had to resist; this was not healthy for either of us. Tate needed to move on, and so did I.

I was about to return to the living room when it buzzed again. This time, it was Victoria. She was calling me.

"Hey, sweetie, what's up?" I answered.

"It's Christmas Eve, Leni, and I'm going to bed soon before Santa comes. I just wanted to say Merry Christmas. I'll be too busy tomorrow opening presents, so I won't be able to call you then."

I felt a lump form at the back of my throat, "That's so thoughtful of you, Victoria. Merry Christmas. I hope Santa brings you lots of presents."

"Well, I have been a good girl this year, haven't I? I know I already have one present under the tree."

"Oh, really? How exciting. Who's it from?"

"It's from mommy," she replied.

Suddenly, I felt chilly as Victoria's words shivered icily through my body.

"How did you get the present from mommy?" I enquired calmly.

"She brought it to me, silly," the little girl giggled.

"Is Tamra there, honey? Can I speak to her?"

I heard Victoria's voice trail into the distance, a muffled sound followed, and then the voice of Tamra King. Victoria's foster mom greeted me.

"Merry Christmas, Leni. Isn't she just a peach? She insisted on calling you tonight..."

Tamra was a lovely person who cared deeply for Victoria, but chatting was her favorite hobby, and interrupting her was up there with the most difficult challenges I had faced recently.

Eventually, she drew breath. I seized the opportunity and went for it, "Who brought the gift for Victoria? She said it was her mommy, but...?"

Tamra dived back in, "Well, she thinks it was her mommy as that's what it says on the gift tag. Someone had left it on the doorstep, but I have no idea who it was. Of course, it couldn't be her mommy because, as we both know, her mommy is..."

I ended the call with an abrupt, "Sorry, Tamra, I can't hear you. The line's crackling real bad."

I sat at the kitchen table and pondered.

"Penny for them?" Eric had joined me now.

"Sorry, Eric," I apologized for not having noticed his presence, "that was Victoria on the phone."

"How is she?"

"Oh, she's fine..."

"Then why do you have that look on your face, Leni? What's up?"

I regurgitated my conservation with the little girl between filling our wine glasses and munching my way through homemade chocolate yule log.

"That is odd," Eric agreed, "but you know it's Christmas Eve. Let's forget about everything else for tonight and enjoy ourselves."

I rose from the table and faltered. Luckily, Eric was there to catch me.

"Oh, look where we are, Leni!" He tilted his head backwards as a smile crept across his lips.

I followed his gaze. Hanging above us was the fresh bunch of mistletoe that Roxy had placed earlier that afternoon.

I felt the warmth of his lips caress mine as his arms folded around my body. I melted into his embrace and savored the moment.

CHAPTER THIRTY-SEVEN

On Christmas morning, I awoke to the realization that I was not alone. My cheek was nuzzled against the muscly chest of Eric Brodie.

I should really have been ecstatic at this discovery, as it had been my long-time dream to wake up beside him, and yet I couldn't help but feel slightly disgruntled. Whatever had happened after our passionate kiss beneath the mistletoe was a total blur. I had no memory of torrid lovemaking, if indeed that had been the progression, and that irritated the hell out of me.

Eric stirred beside me, wide-eyed and smiling.

"Good morning," he whispered.

I wanted to run, retreat to the bathroom, check my face for runny mascara, but most of all, I wanted to remember.

I checked beneath the duvet. I was naked; running was not an option.

I turned to Eric and asked sheepishly, "What happened last night... did we... I don't..."

Eric threw his head back on the pillows and laughed.

"We kissed, came upstairs, started fooling around, and then... you fell asleep."

I clutched at the duvet, embarrassed, my cheeks burning shamefully.

"Oh, my God. I'm so sorry..."

"Relax, Leni. It's fine; at least I got to undress you."

I couldn't help but chuckle as Eric twitched his eyebrows up and down, a salacious grin across his lips.

The moment was short-lived as Connie burst into the room unexpectedly and didn't seem to notice the hulk of a heartthrob lying beside me.

"Leni, come down. Tate's here."

One look at Eric, and I raced from the bed, duvet trailing behind me. Eric lay naked and exposed, grabbing a pillow to cover his modesty from Connie, who simply glanced between us and exclaimed, "Finally guys!"

Safely clothed in pjs and robe, I found Tate in the kitchen. He looked cold and disheveled.

"What's going on, Tate? Why do you look like you have slept under a bridge?" I questioned.

"Sorry, Leni, I ran away last night. I got lost in the snow; I've been walking in circles for hours."

"You poor thing," clucked Connie, throwing a blanket around him, "I'll fix you some breakfast."

Connie fussed over pancakes, hot chocolate, and cookies. Tate looked defeated and tired.

"Can I stay with you guys today, please, Leni?" he pleaded.

Connie's expression was pleading too as she tossed pancakes on the stove.

"Okay, you can stay today, because it's Christmas, but I need to clear it with your foster parents later," I added.

Tate almost burst into tears, but Connie arrived with a pancake stack drizzled in maple syrup and decorated with blueberries and bacon, which immediately diverted his attention.

"Thanks, Leni," she praised.

"I don't like it any more than you do, Con; there's nothing I'd like more than for Tate to live with us, but you know the brick wall I face every time I contact child services."

Connie nodded, "I know, but what if no one knows he's here? Can't we keep him?"

"He's not a stray dog, Connie. We have no rights. Keeping him would just make matters worse."

Connie reluctantly agreed. Tate had become the brother she'd never had, and her feelings towards him were strong.

My cell buzzed, and Tamra King's face flashed up.

"Hey, Tamra, Merry Christmas!" I began, but Tamra was not her usual talkative self.

"Yes, and to you, Leni," she replied with an extremely shaky voice.

"Is something wrong?" I asked.

"You could say that. The gift for Victoria signed from her mommy..."

"Yes, Tamra, what is it?"

"It's a human head. A shrunken human head." The trauma in Tamra's voice was extensive.

I sighed with relief, "Don't worry, Tamra," I explained. "It used to hang on her bed. It's a creepy old thing, for sure, but Victoria chose it. It belonged to the people who lived in their house before them. She found it in the attic amongst other things they had left behind."

"No, Leni, you don't understand," stuttered Tamra, her voice sounding more nervous with every word. "She can't possibly have had it at her house because I recognize the face. It's her daddy!"

I almost dropped the phone from shock, my hand trembling as I tried to console Tamra King on the other end.

"I think this is a matter for the police," I suggested just as Eric entered the room, "can you hold the line for a moment while I speak to someone who might be able to help?" Tamra agreed.

I quickly relayed the conversation to Eric, sounding every bit as nervous as Tamra as I waited for his reaction.

Eric looked shocked, rubbing the back of his neck with one hand, a telltale sign of his unease.

"Tell her I'll be right over, Leni. I'll take a look at the head, make sure it's genuine and not some kind of sick prank."

Tamra sounded relieved as we ended our call.

"I'm coming with you, Eric," I demanded, racing to the bedroom to throw on some clothes.

Tamra King was a woman in her mid-forties, with short, curly, auburn hair and green eyes. She welcomed us into her home with warm hugs as though we were family members.

Victoria came running for hugs too and led me into the family room, where two other children were seated around a large, heavily decorated Christmas tree.

"Look what Santa brought," she said excitedly, lining up the myriad of gifts from her particular pile.

The other children, whose bright auburn hair led me to believe that Tamra was unquestionably their mom, looked on happily.

In the kitchen area, a tall, well-dressed, blond-haired man was busily preparing a Christmas feast.

"Merry Christmas. I'm Jack," he said, offering a hand from beneath his festive apron.

"Pleased to meet you. I'm Leni."

"Victoria never stops talking about you, so nice to put a face to the name." He hovered uncomfortably as if socializing made him nervous. I suspected that Tamra did most of that for the both of them.

When I had spent sufficient time with Victoria and her Christmas gifts, I made my way into the living room, where Eric and Tamra were huddled over a cardboard box.

"Take a look," instructed Eric as I entered the room, "it's Chase all right."

I peered into the open container and the content that was cushioned on a mountain of shredded paper. What stared back at me was the unmistakable face of Chase Richards, albeit a lot smaller and more wrinkled than I remembered. The skin had turned a dirty brown color just like the ones I had seen decorating Cora Hempell's armchair.

"Did Victoria see this?" I questioned.

"Fortunately not," explained Tamra, "the gift tag had fallen off, and so I was the person who opened it, thinking it was for me. You can imagine my reaction, can't you."

"I'll take this to the station if that's okay with you?" asked Eric, "run forensics over it."

"Please do. I'll be glad to be rid of it," was Tamra's reply.

We left the house and drove home with Chase Richards' shrunken head sitting in a box on my lap.

"We can't let Tate see this."

Eric agreed and locked the box safely in the trunk of his car.

In the kitchen, festivities were in full swing, and we arrived just in time to see a giant turkey emerge from the oven and take pride of place in the center of the table.

The day was enjoyable despite its shaky start.

"I see you got what you wanted for Christmas," scoffed Roxy with a salacious grin.

As darkness fell, we drained the last bottles of red and waxed lyrical about the passing year.

"It's been quite an adventure living with you, Leni," began Roxy.

"And not always a pleasurable one," added Connie, rubbing her head in memory of the days she had spent comatose at the hands of the man in the top hat.

We laughed and cried as we reminisced, toasting those who had left us so tragically and praising those who had entered our lives for the better.

"Let's hope next year is a bit less hectic," I proposed.

"Amen to that," laughed Eric.

Tate had fallen asleep in his favorite armchair beside the fireplace. I hadn't the heart to wake him or drag him out into the cold night to the foster home he resented so much. Instead, I threw a blanket over him and turned out the light.

Chapter Thirty-Eight

As the holidays became nothing more than a memory, I packed away the last remnants of decoration from outside the house. Noni loved Christmas more than anyone and always provided a vibrant display of flashing lights and ornaments for her neighbors to enjoy. I wanted to uphold that tradition even though it took hours of work to untangle what seemed like miles of twinkling lights.

As I stored the last box in the garage, I was approached by Mr Cunliffe, our neighbor from across the way.

"Morning, Leni. I hope you had an enjoyable holiday," he began.

"Yes, thank you, Mr Cunliffe. What's on your mind?"

Charles Cunliffe was not the type of man to waste his time making niceties with his neighbors; he really wasn't interested in whether I'd had a pleasant Christmas. There was obviously a reason for his impromptu visit.

"Has the Richards' house been sold?" he questioned.

"Not to my knowledge, why?"

"Uhm... I've noticed a light on in the second-floor side window for the past couple of nights. I assumed it was the new neighbors."

"Perhaps the realtor left it on by mistake," I suggested, pulling the garage door to a close.

Mr Cunliffe hovered as though my answer had not quite satisfied his question, but he replied, "Perhaps you're right." He turned to walk away, then turned back, asking, "Don't you have a key for the place? Weren't the Richards chums of yours?"

Suddenly, the image of the key to the Richards' front door occupied my thoughts. It hung in the key cabinet of the pantry, dangling at the end of a passport-sized photograph of the whole family.

Mr Cunliffe was still waiting for me to reply.

"Err... yes, that's right. I do have a key."

"Perhaps you would be so kind as to go in and turn the light off. It's such a waste of valuable resources," he prompted.

The thought of entering the Richards' home again was nauseating, and I felt the color drain from my cheeks and my legs weaken beneath me.

"Well?" demanded Mr Cunliffe aggressively, "can you, or can't you? It's a simple question."

I dragged myself back into the moment, almost paralyzed with fear by my neighbor's request. My last visit had been a necessity in the search for Victoria, and I had vowed never to enter that house again.

"If you give the key to me, I'll do it," he pressed.

"No... no, it's fine. I'll do it." The thought of another person entering that house of nightmares was even more repulsive than the thought of having to do it myself.

If Mr Cunliffe had said anything more than 'Thank you,' I hadn't noticed. But when I finally pulled myself together, I was alone on the driveway, cold and shaking.

When Eric returned to Noni's that afternoon, and Tate had been collected by his foster father, I relayed my conversation with Charles Cunliffe.

"I'll go alone," reacted Eric.

"Absolutely not; we either go together, or we don't go at all," I replied.

None of us had entered the Richards' home since the tragic death of Marie.

Our investigation into the missing children had halted for various reasons, but mainly because no one wanted to enter the house again, even though we knew that the answers lay buried somewhere inside.

"Look," said Eric as we prepared ourselves for the ordeal, "let's hope this is the last time we ever set foot in that place, so let's make it pay."

"What do you mean?"

"Let's go up to the attic where the Hempell's old stuff is; we might find something useful."

I thought for a moment. I was just going to turn out the light, nothing more had entered my mind, but Eric had a point.

"Okay," I agreed, "but any weirdness, and we're straight out of there."

As we entered the Richards' house that afternoon on the eve of a new year, I chanted repeatedly inside my head, 'It's just a house.'

The smell was the first thing that hit us, pungent and vile. Eric took my hand and led me towards the staircase. On the second floor, we stopped outside the illuminated room, transfixed by the sliver of light beneath the door.

"This is Victoria's room," I informed.

"Of course it is," replied Eric nonchalantly.

We glanced at each other as he reached for the handle. It was a now-or-never moment. I nodded approvingly.

The door opened wide, and the light was gone. Victoria's bedroom sat in the shadow of afternoon sunlight. Eric flicked at the switch. "No power," he stated.

"Then how was the room being lit?" I queried.

"I don't know, but I have a feeling it wasn't by anything I can rationally explain," he replied. "Come on, let's get to the attic."

Another set of stairs led us into the room at the very top of the house. The room where Marie had plunged to her death from its only window. The sight of Marie falling to her death from that very spot haunted my thoughts.

"Torches," snapped Eric, as our cell phones failed to impact on the cavernous blackness before us.

We had entered this room only once before, discovering the jars of black liquid that once stood on Cora Hempell's sideboard.

Eric plucked one from its box. The light of his torch searched beneath the darkness of the fluid, but its contents remained hidden.

Then, as he shook the liquid, a solitary eyeball hit the glass. A startled Eric released the jar from his grip. It fell to the floor and shattered, spraying black liquid everywhere, sending the eyeball rolling in the opposite direction.

"Oh, my God, Eric! Who keeps eyeballs in glass jars?" I questioned.

"The Hempells, apparently," he replied, grabbing a second jar from the box. This time, he unscrewed it and stirred the liquid with a cautious finger.

"What the..." he gagged, fishing out a plump slice of flesh.

I threw him a questioning glance.

"It's a tongue, Leni. A human tongue."

We counted the jars in every box, a total of one hundred, containing, we assumed, one hundred pieces of human remains.

"I definitely need to get forensics up here," groaned Eric, surveying the plethora of massacred organs. "We should be able to get DNA from this lot. What's the betting these belong to the missing children."

Our gruesome discovery was sobering, but Eric was right: we may actually be able to identify the children and give a modicum of closure to their families.

I crossed to the back of the room, where a line of shields and spears stood regimented against the wall. I felt a strong impulsion to push the shields aside, an inner voice instructing me to take a look behind.

The first few shields yielded nothing of interest save for cobwebs and startled spiders, but the third revealed a cache of old photographs hidden beneath a thick covering of dust. I pulled them into the glow of torchlight as Eric joined me.

A dozen or more family portraits revealed themselves beneath dried particles of dirt.

The Hempells' wedding photo. Cora had been a pretty young woman and in no way resembled the scary, wrinkled, old hag of my experience. Baxter Hempell was surprisingly pale for a boy born to Nigerian parents. His pallor was almost white, his curly hair blond and his eyes blue.

"He must have been quite a shock," I suggested, pointing out his unusual skin tone.

"Definitely," replied Eric, taking a closer look.

"Quite a shock to his parents, too, I should think."

"Indeed," agreed Eric, relieving me of half the portraits.

We continued to shift through the images to the very last one. This was a picture of Baxter Hempell with his son Byron and another, older man.

"Baxter's grandfather, I presume; he's much older here though." I handed the framed portrait to Eric, but as I did so, the frame and its contents parted company, revealing a cluster of smaller photographs that had been secreted in the back of the frame.

The faces of nineteen young children, boys and girls, stared back at me.

"These are the missing children!" I shrieked, examining each picture carefully. Their name and a date were written on the reverse of each one.

"Oh, my God, Eric. It looks like Baxter and Cora Hempell were involved in abducting and killing the children, not just the grandfather. I bet these dates fit with the dates we have." I exclaimed with a spark of anticipation.

"Maybe," shrugged Eric. "Look at this."

He passed me the photograph. I recognized the face of the Hempell's son, I'd seen the same one in Barclay Thomas's yearbook.

"That's Byron Hempell," I stated. "He disappeared too, presumed dead like the others."

"Are you sure about that, Leni?" Eric pointed to a peculiarly shaped birthmark on Byron Hempell's neck.

"This is Byron as a child. See the birthmark? And this is Byron as an adult, same birthmark."

I studied the images intently. Byron Hempell as a child had sat amongst the photos of the other children, but now Eric was handing me the image of an adult male.

I stared between Eric and the portrait of the man.

"I don't understand?"

"That is Byron Hempell all grown up, Leni. I found that photograph hidden inside another frame."

There was a lightbulb moment.

"Your saying Byron Hempell could still be alive?"

Eric nodded.

"Why would you say that your child was missing, presumed dead, when he wasn't? It doesn't make any sense."

"That, I cannot answer. But I think we may be getting closer to solving our investigation."

Suddenly, the attic door banged violently shut. The window shattered, blasting the room with shards of glass. I shielded my face, gasping and drawing cold air into my lungs. Thick snowflakes began to blanket the ground around us, and the temperature dived to an Arctic level.

Eric pulled frantically at the door. It was stuck firm.

He raced to the fragmented window and called out, but his voice was deafened by the roar of icy wind. We checked for cell service, but there was none, and the batteries on both phones were about to die.

"No one knows we're here, Eric," I shouted desperately as snowflakes hugged my clothing.

The attic was freezing, and we were ill-prepared for such inclement weather.

The situation seemed hopeless.

Eric grabbed one of the spears and dug at the handle of the locked door, but the head of the spear was blunt and made little impression on the wood.

As the storm thickened outside, drifts continued to grow, spreading across the attic floor until a white carpet covered every reachable space.

We were shivering now as the warmth of our clothes did little to protect us from the icy climate. We huddled together, tucked beneath the only rafter that provided partial shelter from the weather, our faces and hands stinging from exposure and our body temperatures plummeting by the minute.

Suddenly, I was drifting, my body weightless and floating. Was I dreaming, or was I dead? It didn't seem to matter. In that moment, I felt warm again.

As I slipped in and out of consciousness, I realized that I wasn't floating at all but was being carried. My rescuer placed me on the Richards' sofa and disappeared. He returned, dragging Eric towards me. Our savior being none other than Charles Cunliffe.

Warmth soon returned to our bodies beneath an army of throws and blankets.

"You're very lucky," exclaimed my neighbor, glancing from me to Eric and back again. "Lucky that I spotted you entering the house. When you didn't return after the light went out, I figured something wasn't quite right."

"Thank you, Mr Cunliffe," I mumbled as the memory of our situation returned. It seemed slightly weird that my neighbor was monitoring our movements, but in this scenario, I could do little other than be glad that he had.

CHAPTER THIRTY-NINE

Eric convinced the sheriff to send a team of forensics into the Richards' attic. The place became a crime scene for a while as officers recovered the jars of black liquid and examined their contents.

It wasn't long before DNA matches confirmed the identity of all nineteen missing children.

The shrunken head that had been gifted to Victoria was indeed Chase Richards. His grave had been vandalized, and his head ripped from its body.

The perpetrator of these actions was still unknown.

Eric had run Byron Hempell's photograph through the police database. Both facial recognition and DNA sampling had yielded no hits.

There were still many questions left unanswered: who had desecrated Chase Richards' grave and removed his head; who had sent the head to his daughter, Victoria; was Byron

Hempell still alive, and, if so, where was he? Finally, where were the bodies of the missing children?

As Eric busied himself in the search for Byron Hempell, Sonia, Roxy, Connie, and I contacted the remaining relatives of the abducted children. We were met with mixed emotions; some families were relieved at the news, others were reluctant to listen, fearing a repeat of the trauma they had barely come to terms with. A couple of the children had no family left, which was the saddest outcome of all.

I decided that in the case of Jimmy Kale, I would take a trip to Bayside on the other side of town to deliver the news personally.

Bayside was a desolate location nestled against the coast about a half-hour's drive from Sweet Water Bay.

I found the Kale residence in the center of a trailer park, a five-minute walk from the beach. The trailer itself was neglected, diseased with a severe case of rust. Some of the windows were missing and had been shoddily patched with plastic bags, there was trash all over the yard, and a couple of malnourished dogs were chained to a fragile-looking porch. I stepped cautiously towards the dwelling, keeping my eyes trained on the dogs for any sudden sign of movement, but the animals seemed disinterested as I approached, too weak to even summon any sound.

I knocked timidly at the door and waited. The sound of movement inside told me someone was home. The top half of the door flew open, almost catching me off guard as a young woman appeared. She did not seem to fit the style of her surroundings, appearing clean and tidy, wearing neatly applied makeup and freshly washed hair wrapped in a towel.

"Can I help you?" she asked calmly.

"Are your parents home?" I questioned.

"No ma'am," she replied. "They's both working down at the boatyard, won't be home 'til later."

"Perhaps I should take a walk that way then," I suggested.

"Pa's out at sea, and ma's gutting fish. If you value your sense of smell and the contents of your stomach, I'd give that a miss," she advised. "Up to you, is all."

I stepped backwards and turned towards the car.

"Anything I can do for you?" she hollered.

I debated for a moment. I didn't relish visiting the boatyard, nor did I want to venture back to this part of town again later. Perhaps it would be better for me to leave the news of Jimmy Kale with the young woman,

"Maybe you can," I replied.

"You best come on in then," and she threw open the bottom half of the trailer door.

Inside the home was cozier than I'd imagined. It smelled clean and was tidy, quite different from its exterior.

"Can I get you something to drink?" asked the young woman.

I shook my head, and she offered me a place to sit.

"Are you the sister of Jimmy Kale?" I queried timidly.

"I am, though I never met him. He'd been abducted before I was born," she explained.

She handed me a photograph of Jimmy posing with two other boys and a couple I assumed were his parents.

"That's him with Grady and Jackson, his older brothers," she pointed to the face of a small, smiling little boy, squinting through the sunshine as he embraced his brothers beside him.

"My name is Leni. I'm a reporter with the Tribune, and I've been investigating the disappearance of your brother and other children," I began. "A couple of days ago, forensic evidence was found and proven to belong to Jimmy. I just wanted to let your parents know."

"Well, thank you for that, Leni. I'll be sure to pass that on."

"Thank you...?"

"Casey."

"Thank you, Casey. Tell them if they want any further information, they can contact me at the Tribune, or they can contact the sheriff's office directly."

I headed towards the door, where a gallery of photographs decorated the wall beside it.

"So many portraits," I commented, stopping to take a closer look.

"Yeah. Ma loves her memories."

I was pleased to see that Jimmy featured in a great many of them; his family obviously cared.

The last photograph, the one closest to the door, caught me by surprise. Three men stood shoulder-to-shoulder, all approaching middle age, a dark-haired one, Jimmy's father, a fair-haired man in the middle, and lastly—most interesting of all—a dark-skinned man with the hint of a birthmark on his neck.

"Quite a family," I commented, hoping Casey would correct me.

Casey stepped closer, "That's pa, Uncle Wesley, and Uncle Curtis," she explained.

"Uncles?"

"Yes, uncles. Uncle Curtis is pa's brother and Uncle Wesley; he's pa's best friend."

A sudden increase in heart rate and a rush of blood to my cheeks caused Casey to question if I was okay.

I passed the moment off as a hot flush and stepped outside, Casey followed.

"Your uncles look familiar, Casey? Do they live in the area?"

"Sure, Uncle Curtis is the county coroner, and Uncle Wesley lives just over there."

I followed the direction of Casey's pointing finger to the sight of a small, secluded island just off the bay. The only thing I knew of that lived on the island was the old lighthouse.

"Are you sure?"

"Yes, he lives in the lighthouse."

My heart skipped a beat. If this was true, then I had just found Byron Hempell.

Chapter Forty

When Sonia and Eric arrived the next evening, I couldn't wait to impart my news about Byron Hempell.

Eric was extremely excited and wanted to head there straight away, but Sonia was reluctant.

"This man could hold the key to our whole investigation," declared Eric.

"He could be dangerous too; you don't know anything about him, and if what you say is correct, his father could have been a child murderer," sobered Sonia.

"What else can we do, Sonia? We have questions, families who need answers," I added.

"I suppose you're right, but don't do anything without telling me. Someone needs to know where you are."

Eric and I planned to visit Tunny Island the following Saturday.

That morning, we hired a small motorboat and headed towards the lighthouse. The sea was playfully tossing us from side to side as we weaved a choppy path to the island. Eric secured the boat, and we climbed the shelf of rocks that protruded from the ocean as the waves leapt towards us, spraying our clothes with salty water.

As we cleared the rocky precipice, a man was waiting by the cliff edge.

"This is private property; you can't be here," he said, scowling.

Beneath the sailor's cap and the hedge of gray beard growing uncontrollably around his chin, the birth mark was still visible. The man standing before us was Byron Hempell.

"Mr Hempell, I'm from the sheriff's office," began Eric, holding a hand towards him.

"What of it?" came the reply.

"I'd just like to ask you a few questions, sir, about your father."

Hempell's African skin tone paled instantly.

"My father's dead. That's all I can tell you," he snarled.

"Your father may be dead, sir, but he may also be responsible for a significant number of child murders," replied Eric bluntly. "Don't make me come back with a warrant, Mr Hempell."

Hempell turned reluctantly towards the lighthouse, indicating for us to follow.

The lighthouse was quiet and warm, in comparison to its exterior. The glow of logs lit the fireplace, enjoyed by an elderly dog that lay stretched out in close proximity.

The man imploded into the nearest armchair as a large, white cat appeared and nestled on his lap.

"Mr Hempell," started Eric.

"Firstly, my name's not Hempell," the man interrupted.

"But you are Byron Hempell, are you not?" I questioned.

"I was born Byron Hempell, but I am known as Wesley Apuso," he answered grumpily.

"Can I ask, sir, why you changed your name?" I enquired.

The man hesitated for a moment before answering, "I left home when I was only six years old. The world believed I had been abducted and murdered along with a spate of other children in the area. My mother feared for my life. That's why."

"Can I ask why you left home so young and why your mother was afraid for you?"

"Long story short, my mother woke me in the middle of the night and took me on a bus to her sister's house in Queen's. I lived there until I could fend for myself. I took my aunt's last name, and Byron Hempell disappeared forever."

Byron—or Wesley, as he wished to be known—was a man of very few words.

"But what was she afraid of, someone hurting you?" I asked again.

"She came every week to see me, until he found out. Even then, she wouldn't give me up, and the bastard took her eye."

Wesley reached for a small bottle of rum sitting on the table beside him. He sipped vigorously, his hand shaking as he tipped the contents into his mouth.

He sighed deeply as if the tipple had calmed his nerves.

"Who are you talking about? Who took your mother's eye, Mr... Apuso?"

"My grandfather."

"That would be Mahru I-w-u-a-g-w-u?" I spelled the name aloud.

Wesley nodded slowly, "Aye, that's him."

"It's a delicate question, Wesley, if I may call you that, but was your grandfather abusive towards you, perhaps improper with his attention?"

Wesley stroked at the white fur on his lap for a moment; then his eyes widened as if the nature of the question had just been ingested.

"God no, nothing like that," he scoffed. "He was an evil man; he had my father in his grip, and that's where he wanted me, but mother wouldn't allow it. I learned later in life that Mahru had threatened to kill me unless my father complied with his wishes, and of course, my father did."

Eric glanced towards me, feeling that we were about to make a breakthrough.

"Wesley, do you think that your father or your grandfather were responsible for the abduction and murder of children?"

Eric had just delivered the all-important question. We waited nervously for the man to reply.

"There is no doubt in my mind that they were both responsible. My grandfather was brutal and sadistic; he would have gleaned enormous pleasure from slaughtering those children. My father took part unwillingly to keep me safe."

There was a sadness in Wesley's eyes as he added, "I can't help but think that I myself am somewhat to blame too. I grew up knowing what my grandfather was capable of, and I did nothing about it. I hid."

"One last question before we leave you in peace," added Eric. "Do you know where they buried the bodies of the children?"

"They are buried in the bowels of the house, in a room beneath a room," he began.

"We know that room," we added in tandem.

"In that room, there is a false wall. It's painted red. Behind the wall, you will find the graves of the children."

We could not thank Wesley enough for his cooperation and promised to keep his name out of the investigation as much as possible.

"Mahru wasn't really related to my family, you know?" Wesley volunteered.

"Really?" I replied.

"My father was orphaned as a child. His pale skin and hair color was seen as a threat to the village, a bad omen. Mahru took him in and raised him as family, but Mahru was obsessed by voodooism and witchcraft. He was a powerful voodoo priest."

"He's dead, though, now?"

Wesley shrugged, "I'd like to think so, but who knows. If anyone can defy death, it's him."

Eric rose to his feet and offered his hand to Wesley again. This time, he reciprocated.

"Thanks for your time, Wesley. You've helped to give those families their children back. Now, they have closure and can finally lay them to rest."

"You never had children of your own?" I enquired as we headed towards the lighthouse door.

Wesley bowed his head and pulled at his unruly beard, "I did have a son once, but he disappeared too. Perhaps he is lying behind that red wall. If not, he will be grown."

As we stepped out into the salty air, a brisk wind gripped the island. The blue sky had disappeared, shrouded by heavy, gray clouds. The waves leapt higher, crashing violently over the rocks.

"You best hurry; weather's changing. Mother Nature can be treacherous," heralded Wesley above the roar of the ocean.

Eric guided me cautiously down towards the boat, one precarious step at a time.

He fired up the engine, coaxing the little boat away from the treacherous coastline, and headed towards the mainland. The boat tossed and swayed furiously, throwing us around.

As I looked back towards the lighthouse, a tiny figure had appeared on the balcony. Wesley, I presumed.

Suddenly, the figure leapt forward, falling through the air, plunging towards the rocks below. It disappeared beneath the frenzy of waves.

Chapter Forty-One

Wesley Apuso's death was reported as suicide, though his body had not been found. Whether or not that was the case, we may never know.

I visited the coroner's office a couple of days later, asking to speak with Mr Patton himself.

A burly, heavy-chested woman wearing an ill-fitting, bright-pink suit and blue glasses lead me through the building to a lavishly decorated meeting room.

I waited at one end of a long glass table in a comfortable leather recliner.

Curtis Patton entered the room.

He was tall with white hair, wearing wiry glasses perched across his forehead. His white coat swamped the frailty of his stooped demeanor; he was much older than his photo at Jimmy Kale's house, pushing eighty by my calculations.

"Good day, sorry to keep you waiting," he apologized through thin, pursed lips. "How can I help you?"

"I'm writing an obituary on Wesley Apuso."

"I see. You're from the Tribune?"

"Yes, and I wondered whether the deceased had any family still living in the area?"

The question was straightforward, but Curtis behaved as though he had no knowledge of the late suicide victim.

"I'm sorry," he began, "but why have you come to me about this?"

"You were one of his friends, weren't you?"

I watched as a tinge of crimson kissed his face. He floundered, searching for a plausible answer.

"You, Mr Kale, and Byron Hempell were friends, right?"

He stuttered, momentarily stunned by my statement. Then, removing his glasses and cleaning them with the hem of his white coat, he answered:

"Perhaps, once, a long, long time ago."

"So, does he have any family, Mr Patton?"

"There's a wife and a son, though I have no idea where they might be now."

Patton was lying; the slight tick of his eyelid and the constant finger movements were his signs.

"Perhaps I'll ask Mr Kale," I tucked away my notebook and rose from the table.

"I'm afraid that won't be possible. Mr Kale is dying in a hospice."

"So, you remained in touch with Mr Kale but not Mr Hempell?"

The coroner looked embarrassed. He produced a diary from his inner pocket and flicked through the pages.

He scribbled on a note and passed it to me without explanation. An address.

I turned to leave, stopping at the exit.

"Cora Hempell," Patton's eyes widened.

"What about her?"

"You performed the autopsy?"

"Yes."

"You concluded natural causes?"

"That's right, old age. She was eighty…"

"Natural causes doesn't explain her missing eyes and tongue, or the stitching across her lips, does it?"

Curtis Patton almost disappeared inside his white coat, his skin turning the same color, camouflaging the distinction between him and his outerwear.

"What are you getting at?" he mumbled.

"Who or what did that to her? Was it you, Mr Patton?"

"Certainly not. I resent the accusation."

"But you know who did, don't you? The same person who murdered those children. Your friend, Baxter Hempell."

"It's not true; it wasn't Baxter."

"Then who, Mr Patton? Tell me, please."

The coroner rushed from the room, disappearing in a swirl of his white coat.

The address Curtis Patton had provided was in foreclosure and uninhabited. There was no mail in the box or any clue as to where its inhabitants had moved to.

"We tried," declared Eric, seeing the disappointment on my face.

"I know we did. It just seems awful that this man has died, and no one knows or even cares."

"There's nothing to say. His wife would have welcomed the news; he never actually told us what happened between them, only that he had a son."

"I suppose you're right, Eric. It just seems so sad."

As the car engine roared to life, there was a tap at my window. An elderly man was standing there smiling.

"Can I help you, sir?"

"I thought I might be able to help you," he replied. "I notice you were knocking at Betina's door, figured you was looking for her?"

"Well, yes. You figured right, sir. Any idea where she moved to?"

The man stuck his hand out, "Cyril Johnson, ma'am, pleased to meet you."

"You too, Mr Johnson. Now, regarding Betina?"

"Ah, yes. She was evicted a couple of months ago. Her son had been living here, then he just up and left without a word. Betina couldn't afford to stay, bills was piling up, and she was forced out of her home. Terrible shame."

"I see. Do you have her forwarding address, or her son's, maybe?" I crossed my fingers tightly.

"Her son, no, ma'am. But Betina sent me this postal card. It may be of some use?" The old man produced the crumpled communication from his inside jacket pocket and handed it to me.

"Dear Cyril, I made it to Maryville on the Greyhound as planned. I'm living with my sister, Addy, for the time being. The address is below. Stay safe, and God bless, Betina Apuso."

"Thank you, Mr Johnson. That's extremely helpful. You two were good friends?"

"Jus' good neighbors, ma'am, looking out for each other."

"That's really nice. I guess you miss her?"

"Every day, ma'am, every day!"

Cyril was preparing himself to walk away from the car when I asked, "One last question, sir. Do you know what happened to her son?"

"No, ma'am, can't say I do. Betina is the one to ask about Oscar."

"That's his name?" I queried.

Cyril smiled, flashing a row of pearly white teeth. "Yes, ma'am. He hated it."

"So nice to meet you, Mr Johnson. Thank you for your time."

"God bless you, ma'am."

Friday evening after work, Eric and I drove the one hundred and twenty miles south to Maryville. We slept over at the Wagon Wheel Motel and set off early the next morning in search of Betina's address.

Down a tree lined avenue, we cruised. The sun was high, the sky clear blue, and the air smelled of freshly mown grass and orange blossom. Eventually, we stopped outside a beautiful period home painted white and pale blue, with roses growing fastidiously along the length of the porch.

"This is it, 3921," announced Eric.

We stepped onto the porch, admiring the rainbow of pretty flowers that filled the yard. A classic Buick sat on the driveway, shimmering beneath the caress of sunlight. It was an idyllic homestead.

A couple of knocks was all it took to bring Addy to the door. She was a well-dressed, gray-haired woman wearing gold rim glasses and a floaty, chiffon dress.

"Can I help you?" she asked eloquently.

"We are looking for your sister, Betina. I believe she lives here now," replied Eric pleasantly.

"And you are?"

"I'm with the sheriff's office in Sweet Water Bay, and this is my friend, Leni."

The woman eyed us suspiciously, "And what do you want with Betina?"

"Well, ma'am, we're here to deliver some rather sad news about a man she knew, Wesley Apuso."

"I've never heard that name before. Now, if you'll excuse me, I have chores to attend to."

Addy was stepping backwards and pushing the door to a close as another woman stepped forward and caught hold of her arm.

"It's okay, Addy, I know who they're talking about. Let them come in, please."

A disgruntled Addy stepped aside and allowed us to enter her home.

"Thank you, ma'am. We won't keep you long," announced Eric.

Betina led us into the living room and offered coffee while Addy busied herself within earshot.

Betina was a much slimmer, younger version of her sister, though she wore the telltale signs of a life far removed from the privileges her sister enjoyed.

"You're here about Wesley?"

"Yes, ma'am. I'm sorry to say that Mr Apuso died a couple of days ago, and you are the nearest to family we could find."

"Oh, my poor Wes. How did it happen?" she asked, genuinely shaken at the revelation.

"Well, it looks like he fell from the top of the lighthouse."

Betina gathered her thoughts and picked at the hem of her blouse.

"We just wanted to let you know that his funeral is on Wednesday week," I added sympathetically.

"That's so kind," she sniffed, dabbing her eyes with a discolored lace handkerchief. "You were friends of his?"

"Not exactly, ma'am," I began. "We only met him last weekend. Eric had a few questions to ask him."

"The sheriff's department, you say? Was he in some kinda trouble?" Betina appeared perturbed at the thought.

"No, nothing like that, no need to worry. I needed to ask about his son... your son!"

Betina fumbled with the china that Addy had placed in front of us, but she struggled to lift the antique silver coffee pot.

"Let me," I interrupted, pouring three cups of freshly ground dark roast.

After a couple of sips of the strong coffee and a bite of cookie, Betina appeared more relaxed.

"Wes was a good man and a good father, y'know. He provided well for us, and while Oscar was small, everything was fine.

Then Oscar discovered his kin, being Wes's parents and grandfather. Wes had always kept us away from them, and he never wanted them to know about Oscar, but Oscar was determined to find them."

"Did Wesley ever say why he didn't want your son to meet them?" I enquired.

"No, not really. He jus' said they was bad people, is all. I never questioned it; I figured he had his reasons."

"So, what happened when Oscar found his kin?"

"That was when the trouble started between Wes and Oscar. Wes was furious; they fought in the yard 'til they was both black and blue. Oscar beat on his daddy something bad. The police was called, and Wes was arrested. I never saw him again."

Betina's eyes welled as she recalled the last moments with her husband,

"Oscar filed some kinda order stopping Wes from visiting us."

"You never found out where he was living or went to visit?" queried Eric.

Betina's eyes welled again as she answered, "I always know'd he was livin' in da lighthouse, but I was too afraid to go there."

"Afraid of Wes?" I frowned.

"Not Wes, afraid of Oscar. If he found out I visited Wes, I don't know what he might have done."

"Do you know where your son is now?"

"'Fraid not, he up and left his momma without a word."

We left Betina with her memories.

"Imagine being afraid of your own son, Eric!"

"Sounds like Oscar is quite a handful."

"I think we need to find him—and sooner rather than later."

Eric agreed.

CHAPTER FORTY-TWO

The Richards' house was overrun by police officers and white-suited forensics. The removal of the red wall in the deepest recess of the basement had led to the discovery of nineteen child-sized skeletons. DNA testing would hopefully reveal their identities and at last bring closure to their families.

We now knew that the twentieth child, Byron Hempell, had not perished at the hands of a child murderer and that his father and grandfather were the offenders. Baxter Hempell had died of lung cancer in 1977, leaving his widow, Cora. What part, if any, she played in the ritualistic slaughter of the children was not known.

We had no information regarding the grandfather, who by my reckoning would have reached the ripe old age of 112 if he were still alive. That seemed a very unlikely possibility.

Byron Hempell, who changed his name to Wesley Apuso, had fallen to his death from the lighthouse on Tunny Island, leaving the son Oscar Apuso as the only surviving member of the Hempell bloodline.

It finally felt like questions were being answered, except for the unexplained presence and identity of the man in the top hat, who still haunted the Richards' house.

Eric had put out an alert for information on Oscar Apuso but had yet to receive a hit.

Connie and Roxy returned to the dating scene. Tate seemed to have finally settled in his foster home, and Eric and I became even closer.

Sonia visited occasionally, but my relationship with her brother seemed to have distanced her.

Life in suburbia was developing into a reasonable form of normality, or so I thought.

Chapter Forty-Three

The last police cars left the Richards' home a couple of weeks later. Excavations of the basement had ceased, and evidence had been removed.

We waited for identifications to be confirmed.

The house, draped in police tape for a second time, stood like a giant mausoleum. Neither daylight nor sunshine could lift the cloud of malevolence that hung over it. At twilight, we closed the drapes and did not dare to glance at it for fear of what we might see.

There were rumors that it would be destroyed, and the area leveled into a memorial garden in honor of the dead children.

No one should ever live there again.

A knock at the door startled me. I had just settled on the sofa with a glass of red and a new book. Roxy and Connie were out for the evening, and Eric was working late.

I peered cautiously around the door to find Mr Cunliffe standing there in his pajamas and robe.

"Sorry for the intrusion, Leni, didn't mean to alarm you, but I thought the police had finished at the Richards' home?" he questioned.

"Yes, that's right, Mr Cunliffe. They left yesterday."

"Then why is there a light on in the second-floor window again?"

His words were chilling even though the night air was incredibly warm for the time of year.

"I was taking my evening bath when I noticed it, and, oddly, I'm certain that I witnessed the shape of a figure pass by the window. Could I be mistaken?"

I hesitated to reply, waiting for his next statement to include the man in the top hat, but it didn't.

"I'm really not sure; it's possible, I suppose. Perhaps the police have called back for some reason, or inquisitive kids have broken in. You know how kids love a scary story or a haunted house."

Mr Cunliffe looked perplexed, as if the words had no significance to him.

"I thought you might still have a key?" he continued.

I hesitated again, my body language almost answering for me.

"I will go myself if you give me the key," he added.

I could not afford another dead neighbor on my conscience, and though the idea of entering the Richards' home again was nauseating, Mr Cunliffe was not the type of man to take 'no' for an answer. However, I could not allow him to enter the house alone.

"I'll sort it," I sighed deeply as Mr Cunliffe departed.

Grabbing my zipper and sneakers, and with the house keys, torch, and cell phone secured in my pockets, I crossed the yard to the house I had hoped never to set foot inside again.

The second-floor side window was indeed illuminated, lighting a decent section of lawned area below.

I could feel the air around me change as I reached the house.

With the key poised in the lock, I froze. Doubts flooded my thoughts as I trembled uncontrollably. "Pull yourself together, Leni. Straight in, light off, straight out. Easy!" I muttered.

I had just summoned enough belief to go for it when my cell bleeped loudly. I dropped the key, sending it bouncing out of sight down the stone steps and beyond.

"Shit!"

I scolded myself for being so jittery and, as a consequence, losing the key.

The cell bleeped again.

"Call me, Leni, it's urgent!" lit the screen. The sender was Tamra King.

I dialed and waited.

"Oh, my God, Leni. Thank God. Victoria is missing."

My heart skipped a beat.

"What do you mean by missing?" I checked the time, 9:15. "Shouldn't she be in bed already?"

"Yes, and she was. I went to check on her like always, but her bed is empty. I don't know what to do."

Tamra was hysterical, her words bleeding into each other as she rambled.

"Okay, listen. I'll call Eric and get him to meet me at your house."

Eric was homeward bound when I reached him. He detoured towards the King's house as I relayed Tamra's desperate call.

"I'll be there soon," I promised, "just need to find the Richards' keys."

"What are you doing with the Richards' keys? Please don't tell me you were going back into that house?"

I couldn't deny my intention, but the light on the second floor would have to wait. Victoria was more important than Mr Cunliffe's concern over power wastage.

I searched the lawn, flashing torchlight hastily across the grass and following the direction the key had headed. It was hopeless; the key was playing hide and go seek, and I didn't have time to join in the game. I'd go back in the morning; I was sure to find it then with the help of a little daylight.

When I reached the Kings' home, Eric was already there questioning Tamra.

"Okay, so Victoria was wearing princess pajamas, pink and purple?"

"Yes, her favorite colors," sobbed the foster mom.

"So, you put her to bed as usual, went to check on her, and that's when you discovered she was gone?"

"Yes, but she can't be gone, can she; she must be somewhere in the house," stated Tamra.

"What makes you say that?" questioned Eric.

"Well, wouldn't there be signs of a break-in? Something to tell us that we'd had an intruder?"

"Does she ever sleepwalk?"

"She never has before, but I suppose she could, right? That's the answer; she could be wandering the neighborhood. We need to go look for her." Jack was there now, hugging his wife, as hysteria was controlling her emotions.

Eric glanced towards me and shrugged. He didn't believe Victoria was sleepwalking the streets of Crowther's Beach any more than I did.

"Let's take a look at her bedroom," he said and nodded for me to follow him, allowing the Kings a little alone time.

The modest little bedroom housed a museum of dolls and teddy bears, her favorite blue one sitting in pride of place at the head of the bed.

A night light projected twinkling stars across the ceiling, dancing repeatedly on rotation.

The window was slightly open, and a cool breeze teased at the drapes.

Eric looked out, "It's a fair drop to the ground," he declared, shaking his head dismissively.

Outside, beneath Victoria's window, the heel of a shoe had left a tidy imprint in the soil.

"Looks like someone was out here; I'd say a man from the size of the print," deduced Eric out of earshot of Tamra, who was now pacing erratically in front of the living room window.

"You've checked everywhere, right, Tamra?" demanded Eric.

"Everywhere I can think of: the house, the neighborhood. I don't know where else to look."

Tamra was too distraught to make any more sense.

Jack, who appeared surprisingly calm, explained that Victoria had developed an unhealthy fixation on her real mom visiting the house.

"How often did this happen?" I quizzed.

"It began around the Christmas holidays when someone had left that shrunken head on the doorstep. Victoria believed it was a gift from her mom."

"She knows her mom's dead though, right?"

"She does, but to process that fact, she conjures images. She believes she sees her mom, and that she visits her."

"You've taken her for counseling?" added Eric.

"Yes, grief counseling. We were told she would eventually accept that her mom was not coming back, though it could take time."

There was something churning in the pit of my stomach. An uneasy, alarming feeling.

I glanced at Eric, "What if whoever took her the first time has taken her again? We need to check that bunker at the Richards' house where I found her."

"Don't you remember Victoria said it was her mom who took her?" Eric reminded.

"I know what she said, but did you honestly believe that Marie was the abductor?"

"It did seem out of character, admittedly. So, if not Marie, then who?"

"Someone posing as Marie. Victoria said the person smelled like mommy. The child was half asleep; if the perpetrator was wearing Marie's cologne, she would just think it was her."

Eric reluctantly agreed.

"I see where you're going with this, Leni, but that means it has to be someone close to Marie or someone with access to her fragrances."

Eric's words were disturbing. If his logic was correct, then Victoria's abductor was probably someone we knew.

We left the Kings' in a hurry—we needed to check that basement.

To my surprise, Roxy and Connie were home, and Sonia had paid an unexpected visit, sitting with them in the kitchen.

I explained the situation briefly.

"Need help?" slurred Roxy, drink ravaging her speech.

"No, they don't," replied Connie, taking her by the arm and leading her to bed.

Sonia flashed a disapproving look at Eric and then me.

I sensed the tension, "Hey, Sonia—lovely to see you. It's been a while, and I'd love to stop and chat, but seems we have another crisis on our hands."

"Nothing changes, does it," scoffed Sonia.

"Raincheck?"

"Of course, Leni. I called to keep you company, but I can see I'm not needed." Sonia's tone was sharp. She headed for the door.

"Son, wait," I begged, but the door banged to a close behind her.

I turned to Eric, questioning his sister's behavior.

"Leave her—we haven't time to waste. Now, let's get moving."

A hazy, full moon hung above the Richards' backyard that night, adding an extra touch of eeriness.

In the shadow of the plane trees, our torchlight tracked the path of undergrowth that led towards the dilapidated building, signifying the tunnel's entrance.

An explosion of overgrown vines cast unnerving images of finger-like tendrils, holding the wooden structure captive in its tangled confusion.

"This is it," I stated, slipping behind the one-hinged door.

The rug was already thrown aside, and the trap door stood open.

I led Eric deep underground, flashing beams of light far into the distance, quickening the pace towards Victoria's imprisonment.

"How far is it?" whispered Eric, the coolness of his breath caressing my cheek as he stayed close beside me.

"Not much further, I think..."

In the distance, a sliver of light escaped beneath the familiar door.

"We're here."

I reached above the doorway, fingers searching for the key. "Damn, where is it?"

Eric turned the handle, and the door opened.

"This is too easy," I whispered, following him cautiously inside.

This room was empty. No cages, nothing.

I turned to Eric and signaled towards the staircase. He nodded and followed.

The glow of candlelight signified that we were not alone.

"Kill the torch," Eric murmured, grabbing my shoulder as the shadow of a cloaked figure passed silently in front of us. It headed towards the parade of candles and disappeared.

Eric took the lead, reaching for his revolver as we followed.

The soft flames that allowed us to navigate our direction glowed with a tinge of orange. I touched the wall behind them, realizing that its color was the reason for their warm cast. The wall was red.

I tapped Eric on the shoulder and pointed. This was the wall Wesley had described, where the children had been buried.

Parts of it lay in ruins where sledgehammers had pounded it to rubble, but the majority was still intact.

We rounded the corner behind it to find excavated mounds of disturbed earth, the shallow graves where trowels and spades had searched for skeletal remains.

In the distance, the hooded figure was kneeling, digging and shaping the earth. We drew closer, surveying the preparation of another child-sized tomb.

"Stop right there," demanded Eric, pressing the barrel against the back of the shrouded head.

Slowly and carefully, two hands rose into the air, manicured fingernails exposing the identity of the woman beneath the robe. Fingers closed around the hem of the hood as it fell backwards, and she turned towards us.

"That's no way to treat your sister," she teased, pushing the gun aside.

"Sonia!" I exclaimed, startled.

I shot a glance towards Eric, who appeared shocked at the unexpected revelation, gun hanging by his side, jaw gaping.

"Surprise!" she giggled, rising from her knees.

"What the hell, Sonia... what are you... what's going on?" Eric fumbled to complete a sentence in his eagerness for answers.

"What am I doing here? What's going on?" Sonia repeated, her tone taunting and confident.

I stepped forward, "Where's Victoria?"

Sonia approached, "All in good time, Leni," she replied, brushing the hair from my shoulder.

I had never seen this side of Sonia before. The normally shy, softly spoken librarian appeared bold and brash. I could not believe that mild-mannered Sonia was capable of hurting anyone, let alone Victoria.

Eric had regained control. He grabbed Sonia by the arm and pulled her towards him, then the unexpected happened. He kissed her forehead.

It was my turn to reel and fumble for answers.

"Eric?" His name stuck in my throat. I gagged at the thought of our time together. Had it all been a sham? Was Eric a fraudster who had manipulated a relationship to get close to Victoria?

"I'm sorry, Leni. It was fun though, wasn't it?"

I saw the barrel of the gun point towards me. A shot fired, and that's the last thing I remember.

Chapter Forty-Four

When I hadn't returned home the next morning, the girls became concerned. They called Sonia and Eric, but neither answered. They called the Tribune, but of course I wasn't there, and I hadn't called in sick.

"Something's definitely wrong," declared Connie, "Leni wouldn't leave us hanging like this; she knows we worry."

"Maybe she stayed over at Eric's, and it was too late to call, and she's still sleeping or..." soothed Roxy in an attempt to defuse the situation.

"I think we should check the Richards' house; something could have happened there, an accident... she could be trapped."

Connie raided the box where house and car keys usually hung.

"The key has gone," she exclaimed nervously. "What do we do now?"

"We break in!"

Roxy broke a single pane of glass and climbed into the Richards' laundry room. Connie followed quickly behind.

"This place gives me the creeps," declared Connie.

"Can't say I'm all that keen on it either," replied Roxy, flicking at the nearest light switch. "How is it this dark in the middle of the day, and why is there no power?"

"Probably been cut off as nobody's living here."

Connie produced a powerful torch and bathed the room in a yellow haze.

"This way, Con, keep that light in front of us."

The downstairs of the Richards' home presented no challenge, the open plan layout was easy to examine. Connie flooded it with radiance in the search for Leni.

Up to the second floor they crept, mindful of the uninvited presence that had found refuge there. One by one, they checked the bedrooms, bathrooms, even the closets. At Victoria's room, they stopped, listening for signs of life, movement, any indication that someone else of flesh and bone could be present in the house.

"What's that noise?" queried Connie, pressing an ear to Victoria's bedroom door.

Roxy waited for a moment, "Only one way to find out." She threw open the door and ducked instinctively as a cloud of buzzing insects freed themselves from the confines of the little girl's room.

"What the hell," cried Connie, waving her arms frantically as the noisy intruders smothered the space around her.

"Smells like something died in here," commented Roxy, entering the room as the last insects whizzed by.

Connie raised the torch and flashed it around from side to side. A black mold had engorged the wall behind Victoria's princess bed, eating away the pretty pastel colors she had chosen.

"Oh, my God," gasped Connie as a shot of light poised on the object hanging from one corner of the bed frame.

"Is that?" she went in for a closer look, "It is, Roxy. It's Chase Richards' head."

Roxy rushed to her side, aiming the torch closer. The shrunken, discolored, and misshapen face of Chase Richards stared back at her. The top half of his head had been invaded by maggots, oozing from gaping pustules, gorging themselves on the remains of Chase's rotting brain.

"Probably explains the smell," exclaimed Roxy, gagging uncontrollably.

"Come on, let's hurry up. I don't want to stay here a moment longer than we need to," Commanded Connie.

They followed the corridor to where the stairs led up to the attic.

One creaky step at a time, they ascended. The attic was vast, spanning the entirety of the house. It heralded one window, broken and patched by roughly cut lengths of timber.

"This is where Leni found the children's organs," remarked Connie, eyeing the fragments of glass sitting on a discolored patch of floor.

Torchlight bounced across African shields, spears, boxes, remnants of rolled carpet, and animal heads. It hadn't found the shadowy form that lurked in the darkest corner of the room, but IT had found them.

"Hurry up, Con—it'll be dark soon," muttered Roxy, heading for the door.

Connie was close behind but not quick enough to escape the room before the door banged shut in front of her. She was trapped inside.

Connie banged from one side as Roxy pushed and pulled on the other.

The flash of torchlight disappeared as Connie's screams pierced the air.

"Connie! Connie!" cried Roxy, hammering incessantly against the door. But Connie didn't answer.

Chapter Forty-Five

The room was blurred, my eyes finding it difficult to focus. Where was I? I moved, slightly debilitated by the pain that burned in my shoulder. I moved again, just my eyes circling the room, my sight clearer now.

It was beautiful. Deep pile rugs, sumptuous bedding that I had tainted with an unhealthy amount of blood, gilded mirrors, and antique lamps.

"I know this room," I muttered beneath my breath. "This is Eric's bedroom."

Instantly, the memory of Eric kissing Sonia stormed my thoughts, followed by the gunshot.

I moved again, ravaged by intense pain. I glanced towards the source, heavily bound with bandages, blood spreading beneath the white crepe where the bullet had pierced my skin.

A noise followed by movement outside caught my attention. I closed my eyes, pretended to be asleep, heard the door open momentarily, then close again.

"She's still out of it," I heard Eric's voice report.

I lifted the quilt from my body; thankfully, I was dressed. I reached towards the pocket of my jeans where I kept my cell phone. Of course, it was gone. I scanned the room for an escape route.

The only other door led to a bathroom, but the full-length windows accessed a balcony beyond.

The sun was fading in the distance. Soon, it would be dark. I could make a run for it; I could break free.

I plotted my freedom from the confines of Eric's satin sheets, not noticing the tap of heels approaching. Sonia entered the room, catching me unaware.

"Ah, good, you're awake," she observed. "Here, take these."

Two white lozenge-shaped tablets lay on her palm. I shook my head vehemently.

"They're for the pain," she insisted, rolling her eyes. "If you want to be in pain then fine, don't take them."

I eyed the capsules suspiciously.

"Look, if I wanted to put you to sleep, I would just do it, not give you the option," sighed Sonia.

She had a point, and alleviating the pain might make my escape more achievable.

I grasped the medication and swallowed.

Sonia turned to leave as if she owed me no explanation.

"Why are you doing this, Sonia?" I questioned as she reached the door.

"It will all become clear, Leni," she replied without looking back.

"I thought we were friends? You were helping me investigate the children. Why would you do this?"

"I don't have to have a reason. I don't have to explain myself to you," she grumbled, reaching for the door.

CHAPTER FORTY-SIX

Roxy had not stopped banging on the attic door until her hands were too bruised and bloody to continue. The screaming had stopped, and the aftermath was silent.

She stood against the attic door, hesitating, hand hovering inches from the handle. She pushed down hard, and surprisingly the door swung open.

"Connie?" she whispered softly.

Darkness blinded her, the torch was lost, and the light of her cell was feeble in comparison. She inched cautiously forward, pushing through the fear in search of her friend.

A hint of Connie's signature perfume drifted towards her. "Connie?" Connie didn't answer.

A couple more steps, and Roxy's sneaker hit something. She bent down, her fingers closing around the abandoned torch. A flicker of light sparked momentarily, then died. Roxy fumbled, shaking the dying batteries to life. Suddenly, the attic was glowing as a shaft of light exposed Connie's lifeless body. She was hanging like a trophy on the wall, blood dripping profusely from the empty cavities that had held her eyes and tongue.

Roxy jumped backwards at the horror of her friend's demise, a waterfall of tears cascading down her cheeks. "Connie!" she sobbed, "my poor Connie."

Locke Peters was the detective assigned to attend the crime scene at the Richards' house.

Roxy had managed to haul herself down the stairs, unlock the front door, and nestle on the porch as she waited for help to arrive.

Peters had already surveyed the body, detailed the gruesome removal of organs, and set up a police perimeter around the house.

He then turned his attention to Roxy.

"I believe you called this in, ma'am. Can you tell me what happened?"

Roxy stared at him, a blank expression on her face. "Honestly, I have no idea."

Peters, not satisfied with her answer, pressed on. "Can you at least tell me why you broke into this house?"

"You're not going to believe me, detective," she sighed. "It's a very long story, and I'm so very tired right now."

Peters mellowed and directed an officer to escort Roxy home.

"I'll visit you tomorrow, and I expect answers," he hollered.

Roxy crashed on the sofa and slept. Even then, she was haunted by the mutilated face of her friend. Now, she had one friend dead and one still missing.

As promised, Detective Peters arrived bright and early the following morning. Police forensics and officers still plagued the Richards' house as news of the tragedy circulated around the neighborhood.

"Did you sleep?" queried Peters as the bedraggled figure of Roxy appeared at the door. Streaks of mascara lined her cheeks, her eyes were bloodshot from crying, and a nest of unbrushed hair answered his question.

"Nice house. You live alone?"

Roxy reached for the coffee and poured.

"Me and two friends," she answered, eyeing the detective from the rim of her mug.

"Go ahead, ask your questions. I can't promise the answers will make sense, but I'll give you the truth."

Peters settled at the table and pulled out his notebook.

"Let's start with why you were in the house?"

CHAPTER FORTY-SEVEN

As darkness fell, I waited for the sounds in the house to silence.

The painkillers had worked effectively, and I was able to move without the intrusion of excruciating pain.

I sat on the side of the bed, my head still dizzy, the after-effects of the bullet that pierced my shoulder, forcing me to hit the ground hard.

I had to make my escape now before the opiates wore off. At most, I had a small window of opportunity, maybe only a couple of hours. As the room came into focus, I staggered from the bed to the glass doors, pulling them aside with more than a little difficulty. The night air felt cool and fresh. The moon was full, providing just enough light to aid my escape.

The balcony was going to be tricky. I positioned myself at the edge and climbed over, wedging a bare foot between the metal rails that decorated it. I lowered my body down as quietly as I could, but the shoulder wound had weakened my grip, and I dropped with a humiliating crash to the sandy earth below.

Blood was seeping from the bandages; the strain had been too much. I climbed to my feet and dived into the nearest bush as Eric's duplex glowed with light.

I heard his voice on the balcony and the sound of running as he and Sonia headed into the darkness. They split in opposite directions, and the night fell silent again.

I waited briefly in the thorny undergrowth until I was certain I was alone. I fought the sharpness of the bush as it ripped at my clothes and pierced my skin, leaving another blood trail where I sat. I had to get moving, but the sound of returning footsteps changed my mind.

"She can't have gotten far," Sonia commented.

"Far or not, she's gone. I told you we should have taken her straight to the lighthouse," replied a disgruntled Eric.

My ears pricked at the mention of the lighthouse. Is that where Victoria was being held? I needed to raise the alarm before it was too late. I needed to get to a phone.

It must have been a good hour before the lights extinguished in Eric's apartment. I was plagued with scratches and bleeding wounds, and the pain in my shoulder had returned. I left the bush cautiously and headed towards distant lights.

Suddenly, I recognized the area as I stood at the foot of Barclay Thomas's litter-strewn driveway. I banged at his door with the ferocity of a crazy person, knowing that in doing so, I exposed myself to being shot again.

Fortunately, Barclay did not yield a firearm as he edged the door ajar.

"Can I help you?" he exclaimed, not recognizing me.

"Please, can I use your phone, Mr Thomas?"

Immediately, Barclay swung the door backwards and helped me into the living room as recognition flashed across his face.

"Mary! What has happened? Why are you bleeding and running around barefoot at this hour of the night?" he asked, recalling the fake name I had given him.

"It's a long story. I just need to use your phone, please.

Roxy was overjoyed to hear my voice, "Leni, thank God! I was so worried about you," she declared.

"I'm okay, just a little banged up, but that doesn't matter right now. Can you come get me? We need to go to the lighthouse. I'll explain on the way."

Roxy had a cacophony of questions that I refused to acknowledge.

"Just hurry. I'm at Barclay Thomas' house."

I texted the address and begged Barclay for painkillers while I waited for Roxy to arrive.

In no time at all, the beep of a horn exploded outside. I dragged my aching, painful body across the yard and into the arms of my best friend.

"Okay, are you?" retorted Roxy sarcastically, "What the hell happened?"

I slumped onto the back seat with relief. The passenger seat was occupied by a man I didn't know.

"Where's Connie?" I queried, expecting her to be sitting there, sporting her signature worried expression.

The gaze between the man and Roxy told me something was wrong.

"Roxy, where's Con? Why isn't she here?" I begged.

The tears that welled in Roxy's eyes told me something was very wrong.

"Is she hurt? Is she missing?"

Nothing could have prepared me for the truth. The thought of never seeing Connie again was overwhelming. I screamed uncontrollably.

I was so distraught that the stranger took my hand. The warmth that radiated from his touch was comforting.

"Who are you?" I questioned as the tears dried.

"I'm Detective Peters; you can call me Locke," he answered calmly.

"He came about Connie," Roxy explained, "so I told him you were missing, and then you called, and now he's here... to help us."

There was a kindness about him, gentle eyes and an amazing smile.

"Now, explain to me why we're going to the lighthouse in the middle of the night?" queried Roxy.

I told the lengthy story, dissecting it into relevant parts for ease.

"So, you think Victoria is there?"

"Yes. I'm sure of it."

"And it was Eric and Sonia who did this to you?"

"Yes. I think they've been playing us, Rox, to get to Victoria. Sonia was preparing a grave for her. I think they're going to kill her."

The questions were overwhelming, but I couldn't concentrate enough to answer them. I could only think of saving Victoria.

The ocean was particularly cantankerous, and even boarding the boat was hazardous. We bounced insignificantly in its vastness, struggling to navigate its power as we tossed and swayed through the undulating swell.

The lighthouse was cloaked in darkness, save for the sweeping beacon that circled its perimeter.

"It's pretty unlikely that anyone would be here," stated the detective as he wrestled to secure the boat. "How sure are you that this is the right place?"

"I'm sure," I declared, shouting to be heard above the battering sounds of the waves.

"Okay, stay here while I take a look around," he demanded.

"Not a chance!" I replied defiantly. "If Victoria is in there, she will need me. I'm coming with you,"

"Me too," added Roxy, stepping cautiously from the restless vessel.

Negotiating the rocks was difficult with only one usable arm, but the thought of Victoria Richards' sweet little face enhanced my determination.

We stood for a moment, mere shadows at the foot of the towering lighthouse. Detective Peters had tried to request backup, but neither his radio nor his cell phone was working in the remoteness of Tunny Island. We were on our own.

"The main entrance is that way," I pointed.

"At least let me go first," instructed Peters, moving ahead of us, "stay behind me at all times."

The door to the lighthouse stood ajar, only the tiniest flicker of light inviting us to enter.

Peters pushed the door wider and stepped inside, his gun at the ready.

The room where I had interviewed Wesley Apuso with Eric by my side stood empty. A dying fire provided the light source and a modicum of warmth.

"What's up there?" questioned Peters, pointing towards the first step of a spiral staircase.

"I really have no idea, but I guess it's more living space. I've never been further than this room before."

We edged towards the gray, stone steps and moved in formation as Peters cleared each move with a signal that it was safe to follow.

At the top of the first set of stairs was a kitchen area. The smell of rotting food was overpowering, and the sight of infestation a poignant reminder that Wesley Apuso was no longer around.

The next floor opened into a bedroom. The sheets were crumpled where Wesley's body had lain for the last time, his glasses and an open book at his bedside still sitting where he had left them.

Another flight up and into a storeroom, overpowered by boxes of canned foods and supplies.

"We must be nearing the top," whispered Peters as he climbed again.

Two more floors empty, and then we reached the pinnacle, the lifesaving light and the balcony that surrounded it.

"There's no one here," declared the detective, stepping out into the blustery sea air.

I felt devastated, disappointment and pain clutching my body, neither bearable.

We descended the lighthouse quickly, pausing beside the fireplace where only ashes now remained.

Suddenly, as if from nowhere, a large white cat crossed the room and disappeared through an unexplored doorway.

"That's Wesley's cat," I informed. "It was sitting on his knee the last time I was here."

"So, how is it surviving? Who's feeding it, and who lit the fire?" Roxy's questions were extremely relevant.

Peters followed the route of the cat without saying a word. Through the doorway, we met more stone steps, this time spiraling down beneath the lighthouse.

Cautiously, we descended until the faint sound of voices could be heard in the darkness beyond.

Peters' expression turned serious as we stopped and listened.

I could hear Eric's voice in the distance. I nodded towards Peters, indicating that we had found what we were looking for. He reached for the handle, gun aloft as he burst into the room and shouted, "Freeze!"

Chapter Forty-Eight

The room was large and well-lit, hosting a group of people shrouded in dark robes at its center. They circled a stone table where the bare legs of a child were visible. They hid their identity in oversized hoods and chanted incessantly, as if our presence was not known.

"I said freeze!" repeated the detective loudly.

One hooded head raised upwards and turned towards us, while the rest continued their vigil.

"Remove your hood," commanded Peters, but the hood remained in place.

Above the hum of repetition, a blood-curdling voice cried out, "Praise me! Praise me!"

The chanting ceased instantly as the glint of a blade rose into the air and hovered.

"They're going to kill her," I cried, to which all hooded heads rose upwards, and all figures turned towards me.

Immediately, I recognized Eric and Sonia, but the remaining faces still hid in the shadow of the dark robes.

"Reveal yourselves," I cried angrily.

The figure wielding the knife lunged forward, a single shot was fired, and the figure dropped to the floor.

The group stepped forward as Peters aimed his gun from one to the other. He was outnumbered, but fortunately, he had the firearm.

A flash of metal caught my eye as it hurtled through the air, striking Peters in the chest.

He slumped to the floor, a river of blood instantly staining his clothes, dripping to freedom on the stone beneath him.

I glanced from Peters to Roxy and, grabbing her arm, pulled her towards the door. I was slow though, encumbered by pain and desperately weak.

The door slammed before we reached it, Eric's hand prohibiting our escape. Roxy was trembling beside me. I couldn't lose another friend. I made a dash for the knife embedded in Peters' lifeless body. A boot stopped me, kicking away my hand with such force that the bones cracked beneath it.

"I'll take that," said the voice.

I recognized it, looking up towards the hooded figure as Charles Cunliffe stared back at me.

"Mr Cunliffe?" exclaimed Roxy with an expression of disbelief.

Cunliffe smirked as he retrieved the knife. I moved past him towards the stone table where the tiny, helpless body of Victoria Richards lay. She was unconscious, unaware of her imminent slaughter.

Roxy moved to touch her.

"Leave her!" bellowed a voice. A figure moved forward and removed his hood.

It was my turn to express disbelief, as standing before me was Wesley Apuso.

"I thought you were..." I stammered."

"Dead?" he scoffed,

"But I saw you fall from the balcony."

"You saw someone fall from the balcony."

"If not you, then who?"

"Does it matter? He was dying anyway."

"Erasmus Cobb?"

Wesley smirked, "You're very clever, but not clever enough."

"Why fake your own death?"

"What better way to disappear from society than by dying!"

Wesley's words were disturbing to say the least, but not so much as the identities of the last two figures.

The first, a tall figure, stepped forward and removed his hood. Reggie Goodwin, my old college friend. The staunch Catholic, the paranormal investigator.

"Reggie?" A wave of nausea swelled at the back of my throat.

"Reggie, or my real name: Oscar Apuso," he announced, "Sorry, Leni; it wasn't supposed to end this way, but you just couldn't leave it alone, could you? I thought if I played my part and brought in the church to help your friends, that would be the end of it, but I should have remembered who I was dealing with."

"You were my friend, Reggie. I trusted you."

"Trust is a very strong word," said the voice standing behind him. Stepping into view and removing her hood stood Connie.

I almost passed out from the shock. Roxy steadied me, holding my hand in hers. I could feel the tremble of disbelief shaking inside her. I had cried an ocean of tears for the friend I thought brutally murdered, but here she was, standing alive and well beside Oscar Apuso.

"Connie, I thought you were dead," cried Roxy.

"Someone was, but it wasn't me, Rox. Your eyes deceived you," came the reply.

I shook my head in disbelief, "Connie, why would you...?"

Connie gripped Reggie's hand in hers.

"It wasn't planned, Leni. We found each other, and Reggie introduced me to his religion."

"What religion is that, Connie? Satanism?"

"Of course not," replied Connie, disgruntled. "It's voodooism."

"Black magic, you mean," I corrected brusquely.

"Call it what you will, Leni. I was hoping to introduce the two of you to it, if you were more open-minded."

"More like lost-minded," interrupted Roxy. "You're crazy, Connie; you're drugged and manipulated if you think slaughtering children is any kind of religion."

"It's not slaughter," sniffed Connie defensively, "it's sacrifice."

"Same difference," scowled Roxy.

There were a multitude of questions buzzing through my head. Was this a horrible nightmare? Was I going to wake up at Noni's imminently?

Sadly, I was not, and the realization that Roxy and I could lose our lives that night was terrifyingly apparent.

Victoria was stirring now, wriggling and moaning as she wrestled the confines of her restraints.

"Tie them up; we must finish the ceremony before sunrise," ordered Wesley.

Reggie grabbed Roxy, who struggled and wrestled at his grip. He punched her hard, sedating her struggle, and bound her hands and feet with rope.

He moved towards me. I winced at the thought of him moving my shoulder or touching my broken hand, but he did it anyway. The pain incited temporary loss of consciousness, though my hearing remained.

The chanting commenced. I fought for lucidity. The cries of Victoria Richards echoed heartbreakingly around me. The situation was hopeless. The child would die, no one would know what happened, and Wesley and his crazy cult of followers would continue their murderous sacrifices.

Lost in the haze of blurred vision, I somehow felt someone step over me, moving silently, undetected by the hooded chorus.

Then the sound of gunshots spraying continuously above me and the thud of bodies hitting the ground was the last thing I remember, before fading into blackness.

Distant voices grew louder as consciousness found me.

Law enforcement swarmed the lighthouse, and paramedics knelt beside me, their voices reassuring. I felt a hand touch mine. Roxy, I thought, but the hand belonged to Jimmy Kale. He smiled gratefully, his eyes restored, his mouth free to express his feelings. I knew he was ready to pass into the next world. He had just wanted to say thank you.

I felt no pain as they placed me on the gurney, a line of narcotics feeding me comfort. Roxy was beside me now, a cut lip and a bruised cheekbone and a reassuring smile.

It wasn't until a couple of days later that I learned the full truth of that night's events. Connie and Reggie had died of gunshot wounds; Wesley was comatose, having taken a bullet to the head, lodged inoperably in his brain. Sonia, Eric, and Mr Cunliffe, our neighbor, had survived with minor injuries and had been detained in police custody.

Victoria was safe and back in the arms of Tamra and Jack King.

Roxy hadn't left my bedside as I battled a complicated surgery to reposition my shoulder and pin together the bones of my hand.

The miracle that was Locke Peters had survived the knife attack, thanks to the Kevlar vest he sported beneath his jacket. The tip of the knife had severed an artery, and for a time, it had been touch and go, but he made it.

There was one question I really needed answering. "Who saved us? Who had entered the room and opened fire?"

"A man named Barclay Thomas," was the answer, "I believe you've met him before, Mary?" smirked Peters, wheeling himself into my room.

"I can't believe it! Barclay Thomas was our hero," I chuckled. "Who knew?"

The flesh wounds healed rapidly, but the trauma of that night and the events that led to its culmination were to live with us forever.

I asked to speak with Sonia or Eric, but they both declined. I wrote to them, but they never wrote back.

A couple of months later, an envelope arrived from Bay Creek Penitentiary, a letter from Charles Cunliffe requesting I visit him.

I felt nauseous at the thought. The mundane, self-centered neighbor who had lived on Bittersweet Avenue for most of his life had almost murdered me and Roxy. But I had questions, and they needed answers, so I accepted his invitation and set up a visit.

I sat waiting and watching as the guards locked and unlocked gates simultaneously. Cunliffe appeared among a string of inmates, eager faces scanning the room for their visitors.

"Thanks for coming," he uttered, taking the seat opposite me.

I don't think I had ever really taken notice of him before. His receding hairline, his ginger eyebrows, the way the tip of his nose turned upwards, the slight deformity in his left eye, or the way his glasses pinched at the bridge of his nose where red welts had formed. I realized the man sitting across from me was a stranger; I knew nothing about him except for his name.

He placed his hands together on the table and leaned forward.

"I'm sure you have a lot of questions. I want to explain; I need to explain, if you'll let me?" he began.

I checked the time. "You have exactly twenty minutes of visiting time. When the bell rings, I will leave and never return, so you better begin."

Cunliffe swallowed hard and adjusted his glasses.

"Many years ago, a couple moved in across the street: the Hempells. We struck up an instant friendship, and I fell deeply in love with Cora.

When her marriage became estranged after the appearance of her husband's grandfather, I became her rock, her sounding board, her means of escape. The things she told me about Mahru were horrifying, and she asked me to help rescue her son, Byron, fearing that his life was in danger. I was willing to do anything for Cora, and I ferried her backwards and forwards to her sister's house, where she had hidden the boy by faking his abduction and feigning that he was the latest addition to the list of missing children in the area."

Cunliffe paused for a moment. "You see, Byron was not Baxter's son. He was mine."

I shuffled my chair closer at the surprise declaration. "Did Baxter know?" I queried.

Cunliffe shook his head, "No, but I think Mahru did. He threatened to tell my wife, ruin my career, break up my family unless I did as he asked. I didn't want to get involved, but I couldn't risk him finding Byron or exposing my family to such a dark secret, so I agreed to help him."

"Help him how?"

Cunliffe lowered his eyes, ashamed of the actions he was about to impart.

"He was a sick bastard, a psychopath, a murderer. He slaughtered those children in the name of his religion, but I knew he enjoyed every minute of their torture. I could see it in his eyes, the expression of exhilaration as he drove his knife into their innocence."

"So, what role did you play?"

Cunliffe's eyes glazed with tears, and, for a brief moment, I almost felt sympathy. Then I quickly reminded myself of the young lives that had been lost to his involvement, and the feeling dispersed.

"I was the abductor," he sobbed as a river of tears dampened his cheeks.

"You took the children to give to Mahru to slaughter?" The tone of disgust must have been apparent in my voice.

Cunliffe dabbed at his eyes, "I did. I led them to their death. Mahru thought they were more likely to trust me than him."

I wasn't sure I could listen to anymore or look upon the face of a man who had knowingly taken children away from their families, leaving nothing but a trail of devastation behind him.

"If you're looking for atonement, I'm the wrong person," I declared, pushing away from the table in disgust.

"I'm not; I just need someone to explain to my family why I did it," he pleaded.

"Explain to your family?" I scowled. "What about the families you destroyed; the parents left without children, not knowing for decades what became of them?"

"So, you can tell them for me, explain, ask them for my forgiveness," he begged, making a grab for my hand.

I recoiled, avoiding his touch, nauseated by his self-pity. "I will not," I hissed. "I will not add to their sorrow by describing the way their children died just to make you feel better."

"Please, Leni, I need to repent for my sins," he cried, choking on the swell of tears that drowned him.

"Then call for a priest. You'll get no mercy from me."

Cunliffe sobbed into his hands, tears and saliva oozing between his fingers.

"I think it's time for me to leave."

"Please don't. The best is yet to come." Cunliffe began to giggle, bursting into fits of uncontrollable laughter. It had all been an act. He wasn't sorry for his wrongdoing; he wasn't sorry about anything.

He lifted his head to stare at me, his eyes growing darker as his pupils dilated, the hint of a red glow appearing. Suddenly, he had taken on a different persona. There was a malevolence about him. His hair had grown thick and wiry, his skin shriveled by age, and his voice was deep and guttural.

I glanced around the room. No one had noticed his transformation. Needle-sharp teeth invaded his gums as he hissed and spit, chanting in a language I didn't recognize. He rose to his feet, his shadow growing disproportionately larger behind him. A cloud of gray haze was surrounding him.

I glanced around. Everyone was engaged in conversation, and no one saw him place the top hat on his head or produce the cane at his side. No one flinched as he pulled a crudely fashioned doll from his pocket. He threw back his head and screamed as the first pin pierced the effigy. A searing pain shot through my temple to the back of my eye, my head burning as he stabbed at the doll. My leg gave way, a sharp snap followed by intense pain as the entity moved closer.

I searched for the cross that hung around my neck, the one Noni had given me at my confirmation. I gripped it tightly and, closing my eyes, began to recite the Lord's Prayer. There was a comfort surrounding me, a warm, loving feeling I hadn't expected. I was not alone. My eyes opened to a choir of spirits surrounding me. Noni, Marie, and Chase Richards, the nineteen children I had searched for, including Jimmy Kale, who had pointed the way. Chanting in unison the prayer I had learned as a child, they faced the demon, Mahru, overpowering his evil with the words of the almighty. He struggled and thrashed, desperate to unleash his malevolence upon the room, upon me, but the love and belief of the spirits around me proved too much. The cloud of gray dissipated, sucking Mahru into its depths, and he was gone.

Sitting before me, Charles Cunliffe was still sobbing, holding his head in his hands, oblivious of the demon that had lived inside him.

Had it really happened? The pain in my leg provided the answer.

I left the prison in the back of an ambulance, with an open fracture of the tibia that left the paramedics scratching their heads. I couldn't explain the cause of it; I didn't even try. I was done with explanations, questions, investigations. I just wanted to get on with my life.

Chapter Forty-Nine

In the aftermath of my prison experience, Locke Peters became a constant in my life. He served as my nurse while I waited impatiently for the leg fracture to heal. The surgeon was baffled. He did his best to reconstruct the bones, but I now walked with a permanent limp, a reminder of the battle I had fought and won, and the price I had paid.

We both wore the scars of that night, permanent reminders that would remain with us always. The physical scars healed well. Psychologically, we all struggled to cope.

"I don't understand what happened, Leni. How did Connie, our best friend, become involved?" queried Roxy as we huddled together on the sofa.

"I've been thinking about that too. In fact, it's all I think about when I lie awake in the early hours. I don't think we will ever know for sure, but my theory is that Connie, like

Cunliffe and the others, was marked by the evil that lived in the Richards' home."

"Marked how?"

"I think it happened when he was here that night in her bedroom."

"The night she was knocked unconscious?"

"Yes, that night."

"What about Eric and Sonia? Reggie and Mr Cunliffe?"

I thought for a moment before answering, "The day Eric and I were trapped in the Richards' basement, I managed to escape through a small window, but Eric was left in there for a while before he found his way out. I think it happened to him then, and Sonia when she saw the old woman in my en suite. As for Reggie, it happened when he entered the house and was attacked."

Roxy listened and nodded her agreement, "Do you think that's what happened to Chase and Marie too?"

"The way I see it, the spirit that lives in that house..."

"Being Mahru?"

"Right, Mahru. He needs a host to survive. I mean, the guy has to be close to a hundred and ten years old. So, he possesses people. In the case of Chase, he wanted his daughter, and he would do anything to get her. He couldn't exist without continuing in death the evil he had performed in life. If that makes sense?"

"Yeah, I think I get that. But Marie. How do you explain her?"

"I think the power of her love for Victoria made it impossible for her to be manipulated. Marie would rather give her own life to save her child."

"That's just so sad, Leni."

"Yeah, Rox, it is."

"Do you think they knew they were possessed?"

"No, I don't think he possessed them all, just Wesley, but he definitely controlled them."

"So that's why Connie behaved the way she did, but she didn't even know she was doing it?"

"I'd say so, Rox."

Roxy stared into the roaring fire.

"Poor Connie. She didn't deserve that."

"I don't think any of them deserved it. Wesley will probably never come out of his coma, and Sonia, Eric, and Charles Cunliffe will probably spend most of their lives in prison. In fact, Cunliffe will possibly die in prison."

"So, if Wesley was possessed by Mahru, he's now in a coma, but you met him through Cunliffe. That means Cunliffe is possessed."

"I guess so, but Cunliffe will never leave prison, so that's the end of it, Roxy. Mahru will die in prison when Cunliffe does."

I filled our glasses, and we raised them to the memory of our funny, caring, adventurous friend.

I crossed to the window and pulled the drapes.

Across the street, a solitary lamp lit the living room window of the Cunliffes' home, where Gina Cunliffe now lived alone.

"I feel for her," stated Roxy, realizing what I was staring at. "How on earth did boring, old, balding Charles Cunliffe become a vessel for evil?"

"He fell in love, Roxy," I replied. "He simply fell in love."

Chapter Fifty

The Richards' home fell into disrepair. It was never demolished and became a local attraction amongst the kids, especially at Halloween. Stories of the man in the top hat circulated the neighborhood, became campfire ghost stories, and Sweet Water Bay became known as the home of horrific child murders.

I got to tell the story of the missing children in a special issue of the Tribune, entitled 'Don't Wake the Moon.'

Barclay Thomas became a local hero. He found love with a waitress from the diner and received a never-ending supply of free apple pie.

A memorial garden was planted in the local park, nineteen rose bushes representing each of the murdered children. The flowers bloomed a magnificent array of rainbow colors, Jimmy Kale's being the most vibrant.

Tate turned eighteen and was able to leave his foster home and finally move into Noni's. Roxy met Cara and fell in love. Cara joined the family following a civil ceremony, and now they were talking about adoption.

Victoria continued to live with the Kings. She was happy there, though she visited often.

Eric and Sonia spent time behind bars for their part in the kidnapping of Victoria. Sonia had helped herself to some of Marie's clothes and bought a matching cologne. She dressed and smelled like Marie, making it easy to convince the little girl that she was her mommy.

Charles Cunliffe could not bear the claustrophobic environment within the walls of Bay Creek Penitentiary, or live with the reality of his actions, even though he was merely the puppet. He took his own life weeks after my visit.

As for Mahru, the man in the top hat, it was impossible to say, though whenever a full moon lit the darkness, a light could be seen glowing in the second-floor window of the Richards' house.

I rarely opened the drapes in Connie's room anymore; I didn't wish to be reminded of the horror that house represented, but tonight I peeled them aside and stared across.

The house was dark and foreboding. A chill coasted my spine. The blue velvet material swung back into place, and I left the room.

***

The window lit up and the shadow of the man in the top hat crossed in front of it...